The Spanish Mustang's coat was ivory with blue-gray markings that flashed with a metallic gleam, but it wasn't his color that made him stand out. The horse had attitude.

As he reached the opposite end of the corral, the mustang went from breathtaking motion to a complete stop as quietly as a bird landing on a branch. Then, he waited.

"He's used to being the boss," Sam said. "Dad would have to earn his respect."

"He wouldn't be a push-button horse," Brynna agreed. "That's for sure, but he's trainable. So, what do you think?" Brynna asked as Sam lowered the binoculars.

Sam could hardly wait to take the mustang home. He'd fit in at River Bend Ranch.

"I think you've picked a winner."

Read all the books about the

Phantom Stallion

Phantom Stallion

∽20∾
Blue Wings

TERRI FARLEY

AVON BOOKS

An Imprint of HarperCollins*Publishers*

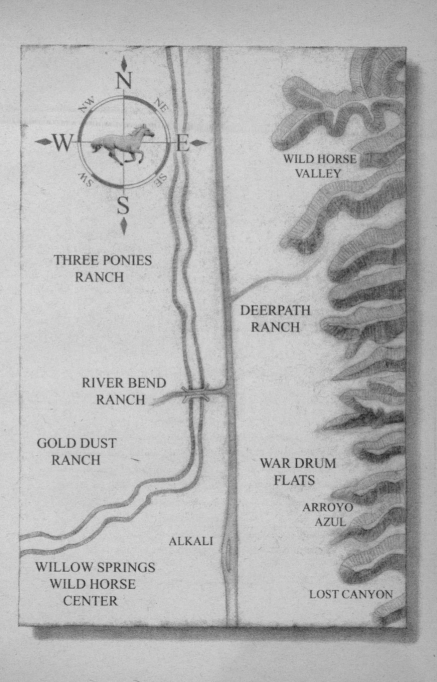

Chapter One ❧

An auburn braid stood out against the black horsehair. Biting her lip in concentration, Samantha Forster tied the strands cut from her own ponytail into Tempest's mane.

For once, the filly cooperated, standing statue-still, until Sam gave her a pat.

"All done," Sam said, but Tempest only shoved Sam with her nose.

The little plait twisted with Tempest's movements, shimmering like a primitive good luck charm in the August sun slanting through the barn rafters overhead.

Sam had read that some Indian warriors braided their own hair into the manes of their horses so that their spirits would mingle. So she'd made a tight, tiny plait at her nape. Then she'd tied it top and bottom with yellow thread and cut it off so close to her scalp that the prick of Gram's sewing scissors made Sam jump.

Stroking Tempest with one hand, Sam used the other to reach to the back of her own neck to feel where she'd cut off the braid. She really hoped it wouldn't leave a bump or gap under the rest of her hair. After all, school started again next week and she'd rather not look weird.

Tempest's small black hooves shifted in the straw. Before the filly turned more restless, Sam talked to her.

"It's just for fun, baby, and to get you used to being handled in any way I can dream up," Sam told Tempest. "I don't actually believe it will blend our spirits, but I do wear a bracelet of your sire's hair." Sam paused as Tempest sniffed the bracelet, almost as if she understood. "And this kind of completes the circle, don't you think?"

Tempest's pink tongue eased out to taste the silver-and-white horsehair bracelet. Then the filly glanced toward the pasture outside the box stall, looking for her mother.

"No, I don't think I'll try this with your mom," Sam said.

She looked past the filly to Dark Sunshine. The buckskin mare groaned and rolled, taking a dust bath like any tame horse. Dark Sunshine was far from tame.

Mustang caution about humans still coursed through the mare, but she'd come a long way in trusting Sam.

Right now, for instance, Sam was looming over Dark Sunshine's filly, double-knotting the yellow thread so that Tempest couldn't shake the braid loose. Dark Sunshine noticed, lurched to her feet, then gave a snort and set to searching for a tender blade of grass.

There. Fingertips tingling from the delicate work, Sam stood back with her hands on her hips to consider the effect. Tied just at the crest of Tempest's mane, before her satiny ears, it looked cute.

Eyes closed, Sam hugged Tempest.

"My Xanadu." Sam's lips barely moved as she whispered the filly's secret name.

Sam felt a fuzzy mane against her cheek and she breathed in the foal's milky-sweet scent.

Then annoyed voices clashed with the barn's quiet.

Sam froze.

"I'll explain it to you one more time." The voice belonged to Sam's stepmother. Brynna spoke slowly, with forced patience. "I've been told to order more wild horses off the range—"

"Fine with me," Dad said. "Makes more room for cattle."

What? Sam's throat tightened. This wasn't the first time Dad had taken sides against the horses, but it still shocked her.

"Which species does more damage to the range?" Brynna asked, but she didn't wait for an answer. "Think of solid hooves like horses have . . ." she said.

Sam rested her chin on Tempest's neck, gazed through the open barn door, and watched as Brynna held up fingers curled in a fist.

"And split hooves, like you see on cattle." She divided her fingers.

"Doesn't matter. Those broomtails don't earn a penny for anyone. Cattle do," Dad insisted.

Broomtails? Sam didn't think she'd ever heard Dad use that word. It wasn't like cursing, but it was worse than rude.

Brynna and Dad sounded angrier than she'd ever heard them, but why?

Dad was a cattle rancher and Brynna worked for the Bureau of Land Management, which set rules for grazing livestock on public lands, so of course they disagreed sometimes.

But one minute, they'd been out in the ranch yard talking about tomorrow's adoption day at Willow Springs Wild Horse Center. The next minute their voices had grown louder, and now Dad and Brynna had begun talking through their teeth.

"—don't even use the same methods to calculate the number of horses and cattle on the range!" Brynna continued. "They count a cow and calf as one animal—"

"But a horse and foal as two," Dad finished. "You told me."

"You have all the advantages," Brynna said.

"*I* do?" Dad asked. "What happened to *we*?"

Brynna caught her breath at that, but she hadn't finished making her points. She stepped closer to Dad and raised her chin, forcing him to look her in the eye.

"You're usually so fair, Wyatt," Brynna said, her freckled face flushed with anger.

Sam waited and watched. Her father and step-mother looked frustrated. They wanted to agree with each other, but couldn't.

Bored with Sam's stillness, Tempest ducked out from under Sam's arm and began nibbling her hand.

"Don't eat my fingers, baby," Sam told her filly, but she didn't pull away. The foal's soft lips comforted her.

When Sam looked up again, Dad and Brynna had moved out of sight.

She edged closer to the barn door and looked out to see Brynna's hands perched on her hips. Dad rubbed the back of his neck.

"Is it worth losin' your job over?" Dad's voice was almost a whisper. When Brynna didn't answer, he went on. "You think I'd abuse this land? Why would I do that?"

"I'm not saying you want to do it, or plan to do it," Brynna said, ignoring Dad's first question to answer the others.

That's probably because Brynna could tell she'd

hurt more than Dad's feelings. She'd questioned his devotion to the ranch.

Brynna shook her head hard enough that she almost lost her balance.

Brynna was just past halfway in her pregnancy, and the extra weight in front made her a bit awkward, but when Dad reached out to steady her, Brynna pulled away.

"Cattle outnumber horses—" she snapped.

"People want beef," Dad interrupted. "I aim to give it to them."

"Consider the impact on the range. All you have to do is watch the difference between horses and cattle at a water hole. Wild horses are prey animals. They run in, take a sip of water, and back off, afraid something might be sneaking up on them—"

"And cattle aren't prey animals?"

"They were once," Brynna conceded, "but it's been bred out of them, and you know it, Wyatt. We've both seen those trampled-out water holes after our herd drinks during a cattle drive."

"You expect those cows to be rangeland biologists like you?"

Sam sucked in a breath. Dad was almost never sarcastic. She was starting to really worry about this fight.

Then, Brynna's face was transformed with a smile.

"What are you thinkin'?" Dad asked suspiciously.

"It's nothing," Brynna said. "Just something I read in one of our baby books. It said parents are supposed to give their children roots and wings, and I can't help thinking it would be good for parents to have both, too."

"What kind of nonsense is that?" Wyatt asked.

As Brynna's smile spread wider, Sam's spirits lifted. She was related by blood to Dad, but her feelings often matched Brynna's.

No matter what Brynna claimed she was talking about, Sam knew better. When her stepmother looked that happy, it involved a horse.

"You don't remember how smart mustangs are," Brynna said.

"So we're talkin' about horses again?" Dad asked, looking truly confused.

Voice filled with sympathy, Brynna answered, "You haven't ridden one since you owned Smoke."

Goose bumps pricked down Sam's arms. Could Brynna honestly believe Dad would adopt a wild horse?

Tempest breathed in Sam's ear, giving her the shivers, so Sam tried to include the filly in the conversation.

"They're talking about Smoke. He was your grandfather," she told Tempest, but Sam's mind had already strayed to another black foal.

Sam sighed. The Phantom had looked exactly like Tempest when he'd been a baby, when he'd been hers.

"Smoke wasn't smart. He was just darn good at self-preservation," Dad corrected, but Brynna wasn't listening.

Brynna's eyelashes were almost closed as she recited the qualities of wild horses.

"And they've got the best feet in the world. They're well adapted to poor-quality forage, which means they're cheaper to feed. They're levelheaded, too, which is why you have your daughter mounted on one."

Ace, Sam thought. Dad couldn't forget Ace.

Brynna wore a self-satisfied look as if she'd won a debate, and Sam knew that when it came to Ace, her own mustang gelding, everything Brynna had said about wild horses was true. There was no way Dad could deny it.

He didn't, but he was one jump ahead of Sam, because he seemed to have figured out where Brynna's argument was headed.

"Don't go gettin' any crazy ideas," Dad said.

He actually shook his finger at Brynna. Sam braced for Brynna's anger to flare again, but her stepmother just linked her hands behind her back and cocked her head to one side, grinning. Despite the bump of the baby beneath her uniform shirt, Brynna looked girlish and smug.

"With that adoption day coming up, I know you'll have plenty of *loco* leftovers," Dad said, "but you're not bringin' even one of 'em home."

"I'm not?" Brynna asked the question lightly,

but Dad heard the dare in her tone and he didn't cross her.

He shrugged.

"I'm going to work," he said, pulling his hat brim lower on his brow as if that ended their discussion. But Dad didn't move away. He scuffed one boot in the dirt and cleared his throat. "About that doctor's appointment of yours—"

"You don't have to come," Brynna said.

"Of course I do, honey."

Sam's worry faded as her father and stepmother kissed.

As their kiss ended Brynna said, "I don't have to choose sides, you know? I can stand here and look clear-eyed at the truth and still love you, this ranch, and wild horses, too."

Dad grumbled, but Brynna just strolled off toward her white truck with the Bureau of Land Management symbol on the door. Her keys jingled as if she were playing joyful music.

"I'm going to go talk with Dad," Sam said, giving Tempest one last hug. "And ask him if he thinks it makes a difference that you're not really broken to lead. You just follow."

Tempest pressed her nose as far out as her neck would reach, and shook her shiny black head.

"Yeah, well, I still think I'll get another opinion," she told the filly.

Tempest sneezed.

Brynna's truck had almost reached the bridge

over the La Charla River when she slowed down.

Halfway across the ranch yard, herself, Sam looked around to see if Brynna was avoiding a hen that had darted in front of her.

Dad didn't watch the truck. He squinted at Sam. His eyes narrowed as if he was wondering how much she'd overheard.

But Dad looked away from Sam at the sound of Brynna slamming the truck into reverse. She backed up in a straight line, right toward them, with her arm extended out the driver's side window.

"She's wagglin' her cell phone at me," Dad said in a kind of wonderment. "What's that mean?"

"I don't know," Sam said. Cell phone reception was so spotty out here on the range, Sam almost agreed with Dad that they only seemed to work when you didn't want them to.

"Talk to Jed," Brynna called. "I'm going to be late."

Jed Kenworthy was foreman of the neighboring Gold Dust Ranch and father to Sam's best friend Jennifer. Sam had a single second to wonder why he was calling before Brynna tossed the phone toward Dad.

It was a totally un-Brynnalike thing to do, Sam thought. Her stepmother must have broken off in midconversation, too. As the phone sailed toward Dad, Sam was pretty sure she could hear someone talking.

Chapter Two ❧

$\mathcal{D}$ad snagged the phone out of the air, but he looked stunned.

Brynna leaned her forearm on her open window and looked back at him.

"What?" she said impatiently.

"It's Jed?" Dad asked, looking at the phone he held in his hand.

Sam wasn't a bit surprised he didn't ask the question into the phone. Dad had decided cell phones were an undependable extravagance, and he wasn't very good at using them.

"Yes. Jed needs the help of a cowboy—you, Ross, or Pepper," Brynna broke off in exasperation. "Wyatt, just talk to him. I have so much to finish up before Saturday."

Handling the phone as if it were hot, Dad nodded and Brynna sped away.

"Jed?" Dad spoke so loudly, the horses in the ten-acre pasture raised their heads from grazing.

Jed must have answered, because Dad spent a long time listening before he shook his head and joked, "That would be the neighborly thing to do, wouldn't it? Sure, I'm sure."

Then he glanced up at Sam. "Yeah, you go ahead and tell her to start ridin'. Good luck in town."

Her? It had to be Jen. Where was she riding *to*?

When Dad closed the cell phone and looked at Sam, he said, "I'll do it for Jed, I guess."

"Do what?" Sam asked.

"Linc forgot to renew his grazing permits by the deadline BLM set and he thought Brynna could 'fix it for him.' Where he got that idea is a mystery."

Dad looked toward the bridge, though Brynna had already crossed it and disappeared down the highway.

"She doesn't give out grazing permits, does she?" Sam asked.

"No."

Linc Slocum was the richest man in northern Nevada and it was just like him, Sam thought, to forget something as basic as filling out important paperwork, then expect an exception to be made just for him.

"So what does he want us to do?" Sam asked.

Brynna had said Jed wanted to borrow a cowboy, but Sam didn't see how that fit with what Dad was saying.

"Jed and Linc are drivin' into the Federal Building in Reno to see if he can straighten out that paperwork, so they can graze their cattle where they always have. But Jed's already rounded up some range bulls and penned them up at the holding corral at Coffee Creek. . . ."

Sam was pretty sure Coffee Creek was a dried-up arm of the La Charla River. When she and Jen had ridden into Lost Canyon, they'd seen some old wooden pens up there.

Sam shook her head and tried to catch up with what Dad was saying.

"Jed says those bulls were the very devil to corral. In fact, he claims he'd rather try to brand a mule's tail than catch that bunch again."

Dad smiled, but Sam still didn't see why Jed needed their help. It sounded like the cowboying part was finished.

"Seems Linc wants to replace all his Herefords with black baldies or Brangus," Dad said.

Sam knew Brangus was a favorite cross of Angus and Brahma cattle. She thought black baldies were like Herefords, only black, where Herefords were red.

Dad was still talking, though, so she didn't slow him down by asking.

"So, Linc asked Jed to see which of the range bulls should be turned back with the cows and which should go to market.

"Since Coffee Creek's nothin' but dust and rocks, and there's other ready water by the holding corrals . . ." Dad's voice trailed off.

Finally, Sam got it. The bulls had been hard to catch and needed a cowman's eye to assess their condition, but Jed had to drive to Reno. Someone else would have to make decisions before the bulls ran out of water.

"Jen's not going to Reno with her dad?" she asked.

"Turns out Jen's mare needs some work," Dad said. "So she's riding out to the holding pen. Gonna meet whoever shows up."

"I'll go!" Sam said. "Please, Dad, let me."

Of course, she didn't know enough about cattle to do the job, but Dad might let her go along.

"What about workin' with your filly?"

"I won't neglect Tempest," Sam promised.

"This might take some time," Dad cautioned.

"If I don't get back until midnight, I'll still work with Tempest," Sam said. She crossed her arms tightly, to underline her decision. "Dad, please."

"Go ahead. If Ross doesn't mind," Dad said. "I'd go myself, but I need to help Pepper deliver hay to Caleb. He's got that cock-eyed hunting guide business started up, and he's taking his stock out and getting 'em accustomed to places like Aspen Creek and Fishbait Springs. He's even feeding them there, so they'll feel easy camping in those places when hunting season rolls around."

Caleb Sawyer lived like a hermit at Snakehead Peak. Sam had seen him shoot a rifle toward the Phantom. Caleb claimed he'd only meant to scare the herd away from the antelope he hoped to profit from, but Sam didn't trust him.

Sam had plenty to say about Caleb Sawyer, but she didn't. Dad had kind of agreed to her riding out to meet Jen, and jabbering about Caleb wouldn't change anything.

Then a muscle jerked at the corner of Dad's mouth, and he looked as if he might change his mind. "You be careful around those bulls, though. Stay outside the pen."

"Okay," Sam said, but her mind was already making excuses. She'd done pretty well rounding up River Bend strays last month. She could ear-tag cattle and brand them, and even though her roping needed some work—okay, a lot of work—she was learning what it meant to handle cattle.

If Jen and Ross taught her how to evaluate the range bulls, Sam figured she would have learned another valuable ranch skill. And if Jen went inside the pen, why shouldn't she do it, too?

"Samantha!" Dad snapped. "No daydreamin' about how you're gonna get around what I just said.

Those bulls will likely be shy as deer, but Jed said one of 'em's got Hazard bloodlines. They're known to be a little snorty. He had to be practically dragged away from Fishbait Springs."

A little snorty. That could mean anything, Sam thought. After all, cowboys said it was "a little chilly" when icicles formed on their eyebrows.

"Okay," Sam said.

Dad wasn't convinced. "I'm tellin' Ross he's fired if ya get hurt."

"Don't do that," Sam said.

Although Ross was the biggest man on River Bend Ranch, he was terribly shy.

Sam released a loud sigh. No way would she do something she knew would get Ross in trouble. That's what Dad was counting on.

"You go tell your gram what's happening and let me talk with Ross," Dad said. He glanced at the rising sun and gave a little grunt. "Hurry or I'll set you to cleaning out your closet and doing that other back-to-school stuff your gram wants."

"I'll be right back," Sam vowed.

First, she made a quick detour by the barn to tell Tempest good-bye, but the filly had followed her mother into the small pasture adjoining their stall.

"I'll see you later," Sam called.

Tempest barely lifted her muzzle from the grass she nibbled, but Sam smiled when she saw the little braid still dangling from the filly's mane.

As Sam hurried toward the house, she crossed her

fingers, hoping Gram was busy.

Sam knew she shouldn't complain. It was reasonable that Gram wanted her to read the first-of-the-year update letter that had arrived from Darton High School. And some time she'd have to try on last year's school clothes to see what she'd outgrown. But it was too hot to pull on scratchy sweaters and long-sleeved blouses, and she wasn't that excited about shopping for school clothes.

She was worried about getting the right things. And, although she'd liked her classes and most of the kids at Darton High School last year, she was nervous about the first day of school.

It was lucky she had Jen.

How many friends were absolutely brilliant *and* cowgirls down to their bones? Jen had helped Sam with math and roping, and had calmed her when she was scared to speak in public and when she was afraid to ride at a flat-out gallop. Sam couldn't imagine going back to school without Jen.

Sam was still amazed by Jen's reaction to last week's secret guests. Sure, Jen had been shocked when she'd learned a stunt horse, his trainer, and the actress Violette Lee had all been at River Bend Ranch and Sam hadn't told her—only because Brynna had forbidden it—but Jen hadn't been nasty about it.

"I'll think of a way for you to make it up to me," Jen had promised, blinking slowly behind the polished lenses of her glasses.

Sam was still waiting to hear what her payback

would be, but she wasn't worried.

Blaze, the ranch Border collie, frisked at Sam's heels as she approached the house. With his head raised and nose twitching, he seemed to scent something she didn't.

"Don't let that dog in here," Gram said as Sam opened the screen door.

At first Sam didn't see Gram, because Gram was on her hands and knees scrubbing the kitchen floor.

"Sorry, Blaze," Sam said. Easing inside and closing the door behind her, Sam took a deep breath. Now she knew what Blaze had been sniffing, and it wasn't floor cleaner.

Even though the windows were open and the curtains pushed back to catch the morning coolness, Sam could still smell the breakfast she'd skipped to hurry outside to Tempest.

Her stomach growled, and though Gram couldn't possibly have heard, she gestured to a brown paper bag with its top rolled down into a handle, sitting on the tidy kitchen counter.

"Help yourself," Gram said, "but don't track up this floor."

Sam leaned toward the sack. She could smell bacon and biscuits.

As long as Sam could remember, Gram had used leftover breakfast biscuits to make fat little sandwiches. Sometimes they held smoked ham or sausage from breakfast, but just as often they were spread with peanut butter and jelly.

The sack rustled as Sam reached inside, and Gram looked up.

"Just one, now," she said. "They're for Ross. Trudy Allen called last night complainin' that she's got flies something terrible around her barn, and Ross is going over to see what he could do to help. With Trudy's bossy ways, I figured Ross could use something to fortify himself."

Sam laughed. Trudy Allen ran the Blind Faith Mustang Sanctuary, and although she was one of Gram's best friends, she *was* pretty bossy.

"I think he'll be going later," Sam told Gram. "Dad's sending us out to sort some range bulls for Jed. He said I could go, too."

"Is that so?" Gram asked, working at a stubborn spot on the floor. "Well, take those with you, then."

Sam had just decided she was safe from cleaning her closet, when Gram called after her, "The only reason I'm not corralling you right now to sort clothes is because I'm going into town and won't be here to help. But, Samantha?"

"Yes, Gram?" Sam said, grimacing at what she knew was coming.

"School's going to start, whether you're ready for it or not."

Ross looked like a bull himself with his thick neck and broad shoulders, but Sam knew the cowboy was vulnerable in ways that didn't show. So she changed what she'd just thought. Ross looked more like a gentle bear than a bull.

Ross rarely spoke and he blushed easily. Sam had read something about cowboys being the "strong, silent type," and though most of the cowboys she knew fit that description more or less, Ross was by far the most silent.

After she'd learned Ross had a speech problem that most kids outgrew, she didn't expect to hold long conversations with him.

Now they were leaving the ranch together and Dad had told Ross to take the new truck. Ross was the first one other than Dad to drive it. As he steered the steel-gray truck out of the ranch yard, Ross didn't hurry.

It took him a full minute to cross the bridge over the La Charla. Sam knew she could ride Ace across in a quarter the time Ross took.

He spent so long looking both ways before he turned onto the highway, Sam wondered if he was looking for something besides other cars.

Still, if she'd been driving, she would have done the same thing. The covers on the truck seat were dark burgundy and spotless. No litter of leather gloves, calf medicine, and chicken feed had accumulated on the floor beneath her boots, either.

A first-aid kit and huge flashlight were clamped under the glove box, and a gun rack holding Dad's rifle was mounted across the window behind her head. That was about it.

"Is that Buddy?" Sam blurted suddenly.

A yearling heifer cavorted away from a group of cattle toward the truck.

Even if it was Buddy, Sam thought as Ross kept driving, the young cow she'd raised from delicate calfhood wouldn't have recognized the new truck.

Still, Sam thought, with her palm still flattened against her window, Ross could have stopped.

He must have picked up on her irritation, because he forced out a couple of words.

"Not her," he said, then took one hand from the steering wheel to touch each side of his head. "Horns."

"Oh," Sam said, looking back again.

Even though Ross had barely glimpsed the cow, he'd noticed she'd had horns, and Buddy was a polled Hereford, born without them.

As they left the herd behind, Sam noticed that none of the cattle had scattered at the truck's passing. Ross drove like he rode, smooth and slow, disrupting his surroundings as little as possible.

When she'd ridden in Dad's old truck with Pepper, Sam had noticed he always took the most direct route, even if that meant bouncing over ruts and flattening clumps of sagebrush.

Ross avoided every pothole and gully, leaving Sam time to wonder if this was the way to Coffee

Creek. To her, it looked like they were approaching the overlook to War Drum Flats.

Suddenly, she felt a prickling at the back of her neck, as if someone had trailed a soft fingertip over it. Her head snapped from side to side. She stared out her window, then Ross's. She twisted around to look out the rear window, then leaned forward to stare from the front windshield, searching for the Phantom.

It was a little late in the morning for him to have his band out, but he was nearby. She could feel it.

Ross spotted the silver stallion before she did. The cowboy steered to the shoulder of the road and pointed. At first, Sam's eyes scanned War Drum Flats, spread out beneath them like a beige tablecloth. She saw a small band of mustangs taking turns sipping from the water basin scooped from the sagebrush and pinion landscape. The two blood bays and a big honey-colored mare told Sam it was the Phantom's band.

Only when Ross said "There" did Sam's eyes lift to the ridge.

Her breath rushed out in awe. The feeling never changed.

Standing between two wind-twisted pines, the stallion remained motionless. No breeze lifted his mane. No eagerness sent him dancing after his herd or pawing at the earth. Silhouetted against the pale summer sky, he stood steady and watchful, the guardian of his family.

Others might have mistaken him for a dash of low-lying cloud or a puff of dust, but Sam sensed the majestic power that charged every equine muscle, even in stillness.

Just then, the Phantom dashed down from his post. He slowed as he approached a stand of salt grass, then circled it at a trot.

It was a strange thing for the stallion to do, but Sam was more worried about Ross. This was no chance sighting. Ross had driven straight to this spot.

"You knew he was here," Sam blurted to Ross.

Her words must have sounded like an accusation, because Ross straightened from his study of the wild stallion. A dark blush covered his face as he said, "I keep track."

There was no greed in his expression. He wasn't like Linc Slocum. He didn't want to catch the stallion and keep him.

Ross steered away from the lookout and drove on.

Silence quaked between them until Ross managed a few more words.

"I don't mean 'im no harm."

It was Sam's turn to blush.

"Okay," she said, but she couldn't help worrying.

Even if Ross only watched the wild stallion for the joy of it, Sam would never let herself forget that each pair of eyes put the Phantom in more danger.

Chapter Three ∽

Sam clasped her hands in her lap as Ross drove down the highway toward Darton, turned off on a hardscrabble trail that couldn't be called a road, then rounded a rocky corner that seemed to be on the back side of the trail up to Lost Canyon.

It was weird to think that an arm of the La Charla River had reached out here recently enough that people had named it Coffee Creek. The entire area looked parched and dry.

When they arrived at the holding corral, Ross didn't announce the obvious. He braked to a stop and turned off the key in the truck's ignition.

As soon as Sam climbed down from the truck, she knew Jen was already there. Her palomino mare,

Silk Stockings, glinted gold in the late August sun. The flaxen mane rippling to her shoulder shimmered as the beautiful mare neighed.

"I'm sorry, pretty girl," Sam said, greeting the horse. "Your pal stayed home this morning. Ace is grazin' in the grass while you're working."

Though she didn't look weary, the mare had already worked hard this morning. It had taken Sam and Ross nearly an hour to reach Coffee Creek. Even if there were shortcuts a horse could take that a vehicle couldn't, she'd bet Jen had ridden close to two hours to get here.

"You need a rest, don't you, sweetie pie?" Sam crooned to the mare.

If Ross was embarrassed by her baby talk to Silly, he didn't show it. Instead, he busied himself scanning the bulls. They were grouped at one end of a small corral. The enclosure was shaped like a figure eight with a gate across the middle, as if it had been designed for just this kind of sorting.

When Sam heard rustling inside the feed shed, she knew Jen must be inside.

Just the same, Sam kept talking to the horse.

"I guess nobody loves you, Silly." Sam raised her voice so it would carry.

The mare's ears flicked to catch the words, but she was busy sniffing the ground for food, dragging her reins along as if she took ground-tying kind of casually.

"Don't go giving my psychotic horse the wrong idea. She already has plenty of her own!" Jen's muffled voice came from inside the feed shed.

Dressed in a tropically turquoise sweatshirt with her hair in long, white-blond braids, Jen used a pitchfork to break apart a bale of hay, then sidestepped out of the shed holding a flake of hay in each hand.

"Hey!" Sam said. She would have tackled her friend with a hug if she hadn't been sure Jen would have dropped the hay in the dirt.

"Hey, yourself," Jen said, grinning. "Your suspense is over, so don't beg."

"Suspense?" Sam asked. She couldn't help noticing how much Jen was blinking as she approached the corral.

"Yeah. If you introduce me to Inez Garcia and Bayfire the wonder horse at the adoption on Saturday, I'll forgive you for keeping them secret from me last week."

"That's fair," Sam said. "But I don't think Bayfire's coming along to pick his own stablemate."

"Just Ms. Garcia, then." Jen continued blinking as she twisted her chin away from a piece of hay that clung to one of her braids and poked her. When wiggling her shoulders didn't work, Jen said, "Can you fix that? I don't want to drop these hay flakes."

"Got it," Sam said, grabbing the yellow-green stem. "Why are you making that face?"

"I have hay dust all over my glasses and it's getting in my eyes," she answered, thrusting her face toward Sam.

With her eyes closed behind the lenses, Jen looked like some kind of tunnel-dwelling rodent that feared the sun.

"Let me help you," Sam said. She lifted the earpieces of Jen's glasses free, then polished the lenses on her relatively clean tee-shirt. "There," she said, propping them back on Jen's face. That's when she noticed Jen's brow was beaded with perspiration. "Aren't you just dying hot in that sweatshirt?"

"Yeah, but I'm wearing a decent blouse, and I didn't want to get it messed up."

Jen entered the empty side of the corral and scattered the hay. In the other half of the corral, the bulls jostled one another and lifted their heads to watch.

Good idea, Sam thought. The bulls would be more willing to leave their companions if they thought they were getting a meal the others weren't.

Then Sam's mind veered back to what Jen had said.

"Why are you wearing a nice blouse to sort bulls?"

Jen glanced toward Ross, but it was clear he was far more interested in the cattle than her fashion confession.

"Ryan was supposed to come with me," Jen muttered.

Sam sighed. Jen was the smartest person she knew, so why did she persist in liking Ryan Slocum?

"I know," Jen sighed. "You don't have to tell me I'm *daft* where he's concerned."

Sam laughed at Jen for making fun of herself, pretending Ryan's British mannerisms were contagious.

Ryan was rich, handsome, and a skilled horseman, but for Sam those things didn't make up for his weak character and unreliability.

"I wasn't going to say a thing," Sam told Jen, and she meant it. She figured that you didn't keep a girl-friend by criticizing the guy she liked.

Then, as if she could get back at Ryan by doing it, Jen yanked her sweatshirt over her head and flung it toward the fence. The top rail stopped it, and it hung there like a bright turquoise decoration.

"Ross, thanks for coming to help with these bulls," Jen said as Ross moved reluctantly toward the girls.

Ross nodded and gave a pained smile. Sam thought it was actually kind of funny that he was more at ease with the livestock.

"It's hard for me to believe Dad decided to drive all the way into Reno rather than do his business online," Jen said. She rolled her eyes and aimed her sentences at Sam, though she stood sideways, including Ross in the conversation.

"I offered to do it for him on Linc's computer," Jen went on. "There's even a box to click on that says something like, 'Permittee failed to apply for renewal in a timely manner.' But no. Dad's afraid Linc's going to lose his BLM allotment, so he insisted on going in to do it face-to-face." She shook her head. "I hope he at least convinced Mom to go with them. She never leaves the ranch."

Sam nodded. Still, she wouldn't blame Jen's mom if she stayed home. Sam knew she'd suffer months of cabin fever before she'd agree to be trapped for hours in a car with smoking, boasting Linc Slocum.

Sam took a deep breath of fresh air and glanced at the huddled bulls.

"They don't look like they're ready for a rodeo," Sam said.

"No, but did Dad tell you about the 'snorty' one?" Jen asked Ross.

Ross nodded. Then a slow smile spread over his face.

"He told Wyatt that bull musta been born full growed."

It was a funny thing to say, but that wasn't what made Sam burst into laughter. She was glad Ross was relaxed enough to repeat the joke.

All three turned to look at the bulls. It only took a second to figure out which one Jed had been talking about.

Four of the bulls were Brangus, kind of maroon in color and shaped like tipped-over refrigerators on legs. The fifth bull was a huge, rusty-coated Hereford.

With a few words and gestures, Jen and Ross put Sam in charge of the gate between the two corrals. She sat atop the highest rail while Ross hazed the bulls, one at a time, toward the gate. Sam opened, then closed it behind each one. Jen stood in the middle of the empty corral, ready to evaluate each bull.

The first bull was hard to herd into the inspection corral.

No way, he seemed to say, shaking his head. Thick folds of skin formed a gleaming bib beneath his chin, and they swayed from side to side as he moved closer to his pals. Annoyed with Ross's hissing and urging, he resisted until Jen kicked the hay. At the appetizing sound, the Brangus' ears, shaped like cupped hands, perked forward.

Like horses, the cattle felt safest in a group, but the first bull was hungry and finally he bolted through. Sam closed the gate behind him.

The grinding sound of his teeth made the other bulls restless, but Jen and Ross took their time inspecting the animal.

"Dad told me to look for weight first. They should be fat after a summer on good graze. And then he said to check them out for the same things a vet would at the stockyards," Jen said. "Respiratory disease, clear eyes, and other things a buyer would steer clear of, even if the bull was—" Jen glanced up at Sam, making her feel like a city girl. "You know."

Even if the bulls were destined for market—for meat—Jen meant. The animals' quiet, almost polite manners made Sam wonder if somehow they knew what was at stake. If they were deemed healthy and strong, they'd go back out on the range to protect the cows through the winter.

The job of inspecting the bulls didn't look that dangerous, Sam thought. In fact, Ross and Jen made it seem easy.

All she had to do was open the gate to let one bull through. Then, when they'd made their decision, Ross said, "Let 'im go," and Sam opened the other gate to release the animal onto the range.

When Jen called, "Next!" the second bull didn't hesitate. He rushed in to gulp a mouthful of hay.

After his positive inspection, he was released, too, but the bulls didn't go very far. They loitered nearby, as if they were waiting for their buddies.

Their presence didn't bother Silly, and Sam found herself watching the mare as she explored the corral area, sniffing the ground.

Silly's search reminded Sam of the way the Phantom had sniffed at the stand of salt grass this morning. Had he been looking for food?

With all the hay locked in the shed, it wouldn't surprise her if wild horses had been down here nosing around. Maybe the Phantom had moved into this place that smelled of humans, looking for the hay he remembered eating as a yearling.

"That eye a little cloudy?" Ross's question interrupted Sam's musing.

Jen moved closer, until she was standing within six feet of the last Brangus. The bull stepped back, flung his head, and swished his tail as if scaring off a fly.

"Looks okay to me," Jen said, and then Ross moved close to the bull with wide gestures.

"Go on, now," he said.

As Sam swung the gate open, the bull rushed for the opening. His warm hide brushed the back of her hand as he hurried to join the others.

One more animal to go, Sam thought as she scrambled back to the other gate. All four of the others were returning to the range. Maybe a rancher's daughter shouldn't have such a soft heart, but she hoped the last bull, too, would be declared fit to roam for another year.

Sam opened the gate and the huge Hereford trotted into the second corral as if it were a bullfighting arena in Spain.

He ignored the remaining wisps of hay.

Slobbering ropes of saliva, he took a deep, loud breath. He pawed the ground, tossing up clots of dirt.

Gooseflesh prickled down Sam's arms as she slammed the gate behind him and imagined roaring crowds, the blare of trumpets, and shouts of "Toro!"

Don't be silly, she told herself. When she rubbed the chill from her arms, Sam almost lost her balance.

That scared her. She didn't want to surprise the bull by falling into his path.

Instead of acting calm and hopeful like the other bulls, the Hereford slung his great head from side to side, snorting as he watched Jen and Ross. He glanced back at Sam where she perched on the fence. His eyes looked bloodshot, she thought, but then he focused on Jen.

"He's sure big," Sam said. Since she was safe on the other side of the fence, she hoped her voice would draw the bull's attention away from her friend.

She couldn't wait to pull the second gate open and get him out of here and onto the range.

"No more meat on 'im than on a well-fed needle," Ross said, and when she noticed he was exaggerating, Sam wondered if Ross, too, was trying to snatch the bull's attention away from Jen.

"He *is* a little thin," Jen commented.

The bull widened his red-rimmed eyes and looked at Jen from under white eyelashes that were a lot like her own.

Jen must have noticed the same thing.

"His eyelashes are longer than mine," she said with a nervous laugh. Then, without turning away from the bull, Jen slid her eyes sideways, toward Ross. "What do you think?"

Sam was thinking she was glad this giant was a polled Hereford, like Buddy. Horns would have made the bull a monster.

But Ross just answered Jen as if he hadn't noticed the bull wasn't mild as a milk cow.

"Not sick," Ross said. "Just older'n them others."

"Okay," Jen said. She sounded relieved as she told the bull, "You can go join your amigos."

Ross jerked his thumb toward the second gate, and Sam moved to open it wide enough for the Hereford to escape.

When he didn't hurry for the opening like the others had, Sam looked back over her shoulder, making sure none of the Brangus had come back for a last hay snack.

But no, they hadn't, so why wasn't the monster Hereford rushing to join them?

Maybe if she opened the gate wider, she thought.

Sure enough, when the gate hinge creaked and Ross advanced on the bull, making hushing, herding noises with raised hands, the bull started forward.

"I'm glad to see the last of him," Jen said.

Later, Sam wondered if it was her friend's words or the breeze that fluttered the turquoise sweatshirt on the fence that changed everything.

Two steps away from the open gate, the bull turned on Jen.

Chapter Four ❧

"Okay, I'll shut up," Jen told the bull, but she didn't sound as scared as Sam felt.

"Wider," Ross called to Sam. "Slam it open s-so h-he hears. . . ."

Sam did, but the bull didn't seem to notice.

Trying to make the bull shy, Jen walked toward him whispering a shooing sound. She fluttered her hands toward him, but as she was about to walk even closer, Ross stopped her.

"Not this one," he said, then rushed forward.

The bull turned, trotting toward the open gate.

Sam held on tight until she noticed Ross's lips flattened together. Was he scared?

"Get off," he mumbled to her.

Sam tried, but she didn't make it.

The great impact of the bull hitting the fence, rather than going through the gate, almost knocked her over the side where the other bulls waited, but she kept her grip and didn't fall.

A glance told Sam the other bulls were suddenly paying more attention to the commotion in the corral they'd left. Tossing their heads, they listened to the agitated Hereford.

Fighting for better balance atop the fence, Sam gasped. In his clumsy rush for the gate, the bull had knocked Ross aside as if he were a toy.

The cowboy was just getting back to his feet, swatting away dust from his shirt, when the bull bellowed.

Without Sam's grip, the gate had started to swing closed.

Sam grabbed it and tried to open it wider. The bull could have angled his body through, but as he lunged forward, he miscalculated.

His tender nose slammed into the gate and his enormous weight kept going, propelling him toward an opening he'd missed.

Sam was amazed that the grayed wooden fence held against the onslaught of so many hundreds of pounds, but it did, and the bull fell, crashing down on his side.

Maybe there was something wrong with him, after all, Sam thought. Could those bloodshot eyes see as well as they should?

Ross scrambled toward the bull, trying to get close enough to reopen the gate before the animal lurched up.

"I can do it," Sam said. The bull was still down. She had time to —

"No."

Maybe it was the thunder in Ross's voice that brought the bull heaving to his feet.

Dust swirled around the animal. He was disoriented. His nose bled and he searched the corral for whatever had hurt him.

He bellowed, as if vowing to hurt it back, Sam thought.

Then the bull dropped his head and set off across the pen toward Jen.

Jerking his Stetson from his head, Ross stepped into the bull's path. He slapped the bull's face with his felt hat, once, twice, but nothing distracted the animal. He veered around Ross and kept going toward Jen.

"Get outta here," Jen roared at the bull. "Go on, git, git, git!"

As she yelled, Jen was edging back toward the fence.

Sam prayed Jen could reach the fence and scramble over before the bull reached her.

The bull slowed to a trot. He kept tossing his head as if his vision had blurred and he was trying to set things right.

Sam sucked in a breath. It didn't matter that the bull had no horns. He didn't know that. If a thousand generations of instinct told him to charge, he would.

Jen was unsure. It showed in the way she bit her lip, in the way she didn't straighten her glasses that had tipped to one side, and in her slow movements.

"Get back over there with your boys," Jen shouted, but her voice quavered.

Should she face down the bull like a matador? Or should she run for it, letting him charge her vulnerable spine?

Sam's brain shrieked in frustration. This was too stupid. She wanted to help Jen. She knew what to do if you were charged by a wolf, a cougar, a bear, and even a shark. She was a cattleman's daughter! Why didn't she know how to react to a stampeding bull?

Sam snatched a glance at Ross. His lips were working, but no words came out. Did he know what to do?

Jen kept backing up, with one arm stretched behind her. She felt for the fence rails. Four feet more and she would have reached it.

The Hereford charged, smashing Jen's side so hard her feet left the ground and her opposite shoulder slammed into the fence.

"No!" Sam screamed.

Jen's boots scrabbled in the dirt as the bull's hornless head held her pinned against the wooden boards.

Somehow Jen managed to grab her tan hat from her head. She flapped it at the bull. He shied slightly, releasing the pressure on Jen's side. She slid down, almost to the seat of her jeans, but when she tried to get up, to plant her boots flat on the ground, the bull lunged once more.

The bull's head ducked, then shoved, knocking her back against the fence again and again.

Jen's right hand reached up above her head and gripped the fence.

She was trying to pull herself up, away from the mighty head banging against her side, but he kept pressing, and the hand holding her hat flapped feebly as the wooden fence behind her creaked.

If the fence broke, he'd trample her, but that had to be better than this mammoth animal burying the top of his bony skull against Jen's coral blouse, didn't it?

Suddenly, Jen screamed.

Sam felt as if something inside her chest ripped at the sound of Jen's pain. Outside the corral, Silly screamed, too. The palomino was galloping, gone, but Sam didn't care.

"Ross!" Sam shouted.

When she started to yell for him to do something, she realized he already was.

All along, she'd been focused on the awful spot on Jen's ribs, where Jen and the bull came together, but Ross was right next to the bull. He punched it with his fists, then danced back, taunting it, trying to turn the animal's attack on himself.

Jen's mouth was agape and her glasses askew. She was trying to say something, but she couldn't.

Do something, Sam's brain commanded.

She grabbed Jen's sweatshirt off the fence and flapped it at the bull. Weren't bulls supposed to charge capes? This one ignored her.

Then Sam remembered the pitchfork in the feed shed. She ran for it.

Sam stumbled into the shed. Her hands closed around the wooden handle.

Knowing she'd waste precious seconds if she fell on her way back to Jen, Sam took careful steps and tightened her grip on the pitchfork as she returned to Jen's side of the corral.

Still, she had to struggle for balance as she clutched the pitchfork and climbed up the fence. Dizzy, she looked down on the bull and Jen.

And Ross. The shy cowboy was doing his best, but the Hereford was numb to his punches. The bull wasn't putting much effort into it now, but he kept shoving Jen with his hornless head.

Sam aimed the pitchfork downward.

Now!

At the same moment, Ross grabbed for the bull's tail. The cowboy braced his boots apart, ready to set his strength against the bull's and pull him off Jen, but the Hereford saw the pitchfork coming down from above.

He spun away from Sam, toward Ross with a hooking movement. When he missed Ross, the bull turned back toward Jen.

"Oh no, you don't!" Sam yelled.

She balanced and jabbed the pitchfork at the bull. This time, the tines touched hide. The bull looked up at her through pale eyelashes. His eyes accused Sam, though the pitchfork hadn't drawn a drop of blood.

Then he was gone, lunging back toward the gate, leaving Jen alone.

Before Sam could catch her breath, the bull slid to a stop inches from the open gate.

Breath huffing, eyes rolling, he lowered his head and sniffed the wood, afraid to pass the thing that had hurt him.

Ross rushed him one last time.

"Hey b-bull! H-hey!" Russ was stuttering out of fear, and though Sam didn't see how she could feel more afraid, she suddenly turned cold with fear.

And then, the bull gave up.

He trotted through the open gate. Ross fastened it so he couldn't return, and Sam climbed into the corral and knelt beside her friend.

Jen was sitting up and conscious when Sam reached her. She picked Jen's glasses out of the dirt. She held them up and blew on the lenses, surprised they weren't broken. Then, Sam carefully replaced them on her friend's face.

Jen gave a thankful sigh, but her face was as pale as her hair and she trembled as she looked down at a spreading patch of wetness on her coral blouse.

"Wish—" Jen began, then stopped. She winced at the pain the word cost her, but she went on. "I wish that was bull slobber."

Sam shook her head. "It's not."

"It's snot?" Jen tried to joke, but tears were rolling down her cheeks. "Sam—" A sob tore the word, and Jen's mouth opened in pain. "It really, really hurts."

Sam looked up at Ross. He towered over them, his face carefully blank.

When Ross said nothing, Sam pictured the bull's head thrusting against Jen's side over and over again.

"Do you think it's a broken rib?" Sam asked.

"Hope so," Ross said, and the two words took Sam's breath away.

It could be something worse. That's what he meant.

The bleak expression Ross wore as he gazed at the range stretching out bare and empty away from them made Sam afraid.

For the first time that she could remember since coming home to Nevada, Sam felt isolated.

The wide emptiness looked dead.

The three of them and the restless cattle were the only signs of life. Sam listened for cars passing on the highway and heard nothing. Even Jen's palomino was gone.

They needed help, but it wouldn't come to them. No, they'd have to go looking for it.

Ross made a gesture as if Sam should inspect Jen's injury, and Sam felt a flash of anger.

He was the adult. He had more experience than she did. Why didn't he do it?

"You—" Sam began, but she broke off when Ross held his big hands toward her, as if they were too clumsy for the delicate job of examining Jen's ribs.

"Okay," Sam agreed. She caught herself whispering, but she didn't know why.

Using two fingers, Sam lifted the hem of the coral blouse, moving slowly and carefully, trying her best not to hurt Jen.

Sam didn't see much blood, but suddenly, she tasted it. She was biting her lip that hard.

Against the pale skin over Jen's ribs, there was an abrasion. It looked no worse than a skinned knee, and it seemed to match the wetness on Jen's blouse. Other than that, Sam only saw scratches. Sam could hardly believe it.

Sam felt relieved and told Jen, "You're really only bleeding a teeny bit."

Sam had barely pronounced the last word when she noticed swelling. Then, a dent. There, in the middle of a rib, where Jen shouldn't have a joint, she did. Sam sucked in a breath.

"What?" Jen demanded, then caught her breath again, grimacing.

"I'm pretty sure it's a broken rib," Sam said, looking up at Ross.

He nodded. "Feel broken?" he asked Jen.

"I don't—" Jen let her breath rush out. Her eyes closed and she moaned, "Yeah."

"Okay, I'm not going to touch it," Sam said. But when she started to lower Jen's shirt, Ross shook his head.

"L-look around s-s-s . . ." Ross's face turned scarlet, but Sam knew it wasn't shyness. It was rage.

All of a sudden he'd started stuttering. Maybe it was the stress or the pressure of being in charge. Whatever it was didn't really matter, Sam realized.

Cowboys communicated from ridge tops to the range below, from one side of a noisy herd to the other with gestures. And she'd picked up enough of the skill to understand Ross was asking her to keep looking Jen over for other injuries. So she did.

"I'm sorry, Jen," Sam said as she searched her friend's side and arms for more injuries.

She found nothing else, but the area over the dented rib continued to swell, and little muscles around it jerked as if cut loose by sharp ends of bone.

"We have to get her to the doctor," Sam said.

Ross nodded. "Bind it," he said.

Jen mumbled something that sounded like a contradiction, but she seemed afraid to talk because it hurt. Still, she was full of something she wanted to say, so Sam leaned closer to listen.

"Tape it," Jen managed to say.

Ross stared at the truck, and Sam remembered the first-aid kit under the glove compartment. She hoped Dad had already stocked the kit and included first-aid tape.

It turned out that there was no tape, but there was a thick elastic bandage, and they wound it as tightly as they dared around Jen's ribs.

Then, despite her moans, Ross insisted on snatching Jen's sweatshirt from the fence and using it to stabilize the break even more.

Ross wrapped the sweatshirt sleeves around Jen's ribs, all the time shaking his head as if the best he could do wasn't good enough.

When he'd tied the sleeves tight, Ross sat back on his boot heels to listen to Jen.

"An object in motion tends to remain in motion," Jen muttered. Her voice held a wondering quality.

Sam and Ross looked at each other, puzzled.

Was Jen delirious?

But then Jen said, "Momentum. That bull had a lot of momentum going. I've never seen anything quite like it."

And then, she passed out.

Chapter Five ❧

For one awful instant, Sam wanted to shake Jen awake. But then Jen took a deep breath and her blue eyes opened.

"I'm such a baby," Jen whimpered. "I want my mom."

The words brought tears to Sam's eyes. She didn't know what to say.

Jen took a shaky breath, stared past Sam, and whispered, "Go get Silly."

Sam glanced over her shoulder. The bulls were nowhere in sight, but she saw the palomino about half a mile away.

Silly danced restlessly in one place, lifting her head, tilting it, then lowering it. She longed to return to Jen, but was it safe to approach the scene of all that chaos?

As if she felt all eyes on her, Silly bolted off a few steps, but her ears still flicked far forward, pointing toward Jen.

"Silly will go home," Sam said, but then she caught Ross's dubious expression. "Don't *you* think she'll go home?"

"Not room f-f-for all, all—" Ross set his jaw, silencing his traitorous tongue, but Sam had heard enough to realize Ross had changed the subject. He was staring at the gray truck.

"We'll fit," Sam protested. She'd ridden three across in a pickup truck plenty of times.

Then she thought of Jen's injury. It might hurt even worse if they all crammed in together and went bouncing across the range, then down the rough road.

"Bone ends are already grating against each other," Jen said, looking queasy.

The image made Sam feel sick, too, but Ross's solution—putting Jen's left arm in a sling so that her elbow didn't flail around and cause one of those bone splinters to puncture a lung—didn't make Sam or Jen feel better.

"We'll d-drive straight to D-darton," Ross said.

Darton had the closest real hospital, but it was a long drive. Sam realized Ross wasn't about to detour to Gold Dust Ranch just to find Jen's mother gone.

Sam couldn't bear watching Jen drive away injured. But if they sat three across, could she lean away from Jen and not bump her the whole way?

Why do you need to go? Sam asked herself. Why not leave the truck cab less crowded and catch the horse Jen was worried about?

It didn't take a genius to figure out how selfish she'd be if she insisted on going.

Sighing, Sam said, "Okay, you two go and I'll take Silly home. But call me," she said, giving Ross an "or else" stare, "and tell me what the doctors say."

The minute she gave in, Ross acted.

"Hang on," Ross said.

He scooped Jen off the ground. The movement was quick but careful, and if Ross cringed at Jen's groan, he didn't let it show.

Sam hurried ahead, holding the gate open. As soon as Ross made it through with Jen, Sam rushed to the truck and opened the passenger's side door.

The smell of the bacon and biscuit sandwiches turned her stomach, and she'd bet they'd make Jen feel even sicker. So Sam grabbed the grease-spotted brown bag and tossed it out of the truck, hoping Ross wasn't hungry.

By then Ross was beside her. Sam grabbed the seat belt out of the way and fretted over it.

She knew she had to fasten Jen's seat belt, but she held her breath, moving with gentle caution. The buckle felt cold to her fingers.

Sam couldn't tell if she'd done a good job or not. Jen stayed silent, just staring at her.

"I'll go tell your parents," Sam started, then she swallowed hard. She nodded resolutely. She didn't know where she'd find them, but for Jen, she would.

The promise made Jen relax. She closed her eyes and sagged against the seatback.

"You," Ross began as he hurried to the other side of the truck.

"I'll be fine," Sam said. "Silly'll come to me, I'm pretty sure. And I can ride her home."

Ross sent a hard stare toward the range.

The bulls were back again, closer than they'd been before.

But not for long.

In one smooth motion, Ross took Dad's rifle from the rack. He didn't graze Jen's head or give much of a warning before he pointed the weapon skyward. Sam barely had time to cover her ears before Ross fired.

She thought Jen jumped, making a squeak as she did, but Sam's ears were ringing too loudly to be sure.

Still, the single shot had done its job.

Tails upright like calves', the bulls scattered in five directions, then moved back together. Side by side, they ran.

When Sam looked away from them, Ross was pointing a finger at her.

"Careful," he said. "Fishbait Spring is—" He

gestured, and Sam guessed that meant the huge Hereford's territory was nearby.

With the rifle stowed and Jen's seat belt checked a final time, Ross drove away. Maneuvering smoothly around the sagebrush and each rock, he took Jen to the hospital.

A nicker floated after them.

Sam was amazed. Parade-trained to tolerate everything from circus elephants to mock gun fights, Silly had stayed nearby. She gazed after the steel-gray truck.

Could Silly know Ross had taken Jen away? The palomino mare had wandered close enough, now, that Sam could see her reins dragged alongside her. How could she catch Silly?

Think like a horse, Sam told herself, *a flighty, nervous horse.*

Comfort and food came from humans. Silly would know that, but those were things she'd learned. The mare had been born with prey instincts even though she was the product of years of selective breeding. And those prey instincts told her that anything as violent and confusing as the last fifteen minutes could be dangerous.

What made a horse forget danger? Once more, Sam's mind circled back to food. She walked toward the hay shed. If she was lucky, Silly's anxiety would lessen when she smelled food.

Sam tugged handfuls of hay loose from the bales and scattered them.

"Here, girl," Sam said. She smooched at the mare and made a big deal of letting the last few pieces of hay fall from her hands.

Moving with care, Silly approached. She stood off as far as she could and still be able to reach the hay by stretching her neck and using her supple, golden lips.

Sam edged toward the mare.

"Pretty girl. You're the prettiest of all the Kenworthy palominos, aren't you?" Sam crooned. "Those snowy white stockings are prettier than Champ's or Mantilla's, and your ripply mane is longer than Golden Rose's or Sundance's." Sam stood close enough now that she could touch the mare's shoulder. She slid her fingers over the satiny golden hide, but she didn't grab for the reins. Yet. "Yeah, you should be called Silk Stockings every day, shouldn't you? Jen's the nutty one to call you Silly."

Lulled by Sam's words, the palomino barely noticed when Sam grabbed her reins.

Gotcha, Sam thought, but she kept moving slowly, calming the mare as she lipped up the last of the hay.

"Let me close up the feed shack and then we'll get away from those guys," Sam said, glancing back at the empty range. "They're what my gram calls 'roughnecks,' and you don't want anything to do with them."

Sam knotted Silly's reins to the fence. Then, once more, she slid a soothing hand over the mare's shimmering skin.

Keeping Silly calm was worth every second, Sam thought. She didn't want the mare worked up and hard to control. Sam knew she wasn't half the rider Jen was, but she had to ride Silly home.

The tranquility seemed to flow both ways. Passing her hand over the mare again and again, Sam stared at the mountains. She wished for a glimpse of the Phantom, knowing he was nowhere around.

If he had been there before, the bulls' ruckus and the gunshot would have sent his herd galloping away and Silly would have gone with them.

The palomino mare blew through her lips and rested a hind hoof on its tip, reflecting peacefulness back to Sam as she eased a hand between the saddle and Silly's withers and massaged her.

"Does that feel good, Silly?" Sam asked.

She rolled her own shoulders, loosening the tension there.

Jen would be fine. Even in pain, Jen had tried to joke. If she'd been dying—and let's face it, Sam lectured herself, that's what she'd been worried about—Jen wouldn't have teased her about bull snot.

"Thanks for the therapy," Sam told Silly, giving the mare a hearty pat. "Now let's take you home."

Once Sam was in Jen's saddle, Silly behaved like the well-trained saddle horse she was, covering the miles back to Gold Dust Ranch with a swinging, ground-eating lope.

Sam glanced up at the August sky. Was it one

o'clock? Two? She hadn't put on her watch this morning and she wasn't that good at reading the position of the sun, but her hunger pangs said it was for sure past lunchtime.

As she approached the ranch, Sam couldn't remember ever coming here alone.

The huge wrought-iron gates swung open before her, operated by remote control. Did that mean someone had seen her coming, or was there some motion detector she couldn't see?

As much as she despised Linc Slocum, his home ranch was an amazing place. The road beneath Silly's hooves was flanked with flowerbeds full of purple and pink petunias. Water sprinkled them so that even in the August heat, their delicate petals didn't wilt.

White-washed wooden fences marked off pastures that held three breeds of cattle: Angus, Brahmas, and Dutch Belteds, which looked sort of like black Angus with white sheets wrapped around their middles.

Another pasture held Shetland ponies, which sprinted alongside the fence, challenging Silly to a race.

Normally Sam would have let her eyes feast on the beautiful horses and she would have searched the pasture for Princess Kitty, the Phantom's mother, but now she just wondered why the ranch was so quiet.

The asphalt road seemed to unroll before her, leading her eyes to the mansion perched on the man-made hill up ahead.

Plenty of cars were parked in the half-circle

driveway in front of Slocum's Southern-styled mansion: a blue Mercedes, a champagne-colored Jeep Cherokee, a beige Cadillac, and a yellow Hummer. Jed Kenworthy's truck was gone, but there were plenty of people to give Jen's mother Lila a ride to the hospital. If she was still here.

Silly's hooves stuttered as if Sam had picked the wrong redwood post to tie her to, but Sam swung out of the saddle and looped her reins through the brass ring just the same.

She had to force her boots to walk toward the foreman's house. If Jen's mother was here, Sam was the only one who could tell her what had happened, but she was afraid to bring such bad news.

She was watching the foreman's house, hoping the house was empty, when Jen's mother came through the door and looked right at her.

Lila Kenworthy wore a white shirt tucked into jeans; a red bandanna was tied over her hair; and she shaded her eyes against the sun.

"Sam? Is that you? On Silly?" Lila's voice was high-pitched, as if her throat was tight with the question she didn't want to ask. But she did. "Is everything all right? Sam, where's Jennifer?"

Chapter Six ∽

*O*fter Sam explained the accident, Lila burst into a flurry of action.

First, she pulled a muffin pan from the oven and inverted it over a cooling rack on the kitchen counter.

"Can't let these burn the house down," she muttered as the last yellow muffin toppled free.

Then she called the hospital in Darton. As she waited for someone to answer, she told Sam she wanted to alert the emergency room that Jen would be arriving any minute with a broken rib.

Trapping the telephone receiver between her shoulder and ear, Lila snagged her purse from a shelf and extracted her wallet from the purse and a card from the wallet. As she read out insurance information from the card to someone at the hospital, she slipped the bandanna off her head.

At last, Lila hung up the phone, brushed out her hair, and muttered, "Linc just had to have those blasted bulls checked out today. He couldn't wait, couldn't go into Reno by himself . . ."

Lila's voice trailed off and she stared into a mirror, still brushing minutes after her black hair was smooth.

Seeing that Jen's mom was more shaken than she wanted to let on, Sam called Helen Coley, the Slocums' housekeeper and one of Gram's best friends. Maybe she could help.

"Mrs. Coley . . . ," Sam began, "there's been an accident. Jen's hurt and on her way to the hospital—" but she'd barely explained before the woman interrupted.

"I'll be right there," Mrs. Coley said, and Sam heard a key jingle off a hook and a door slam before the phone clicked off.

"Where *is* my purse?" Lila said, glancing everywhere except the middle of the kitchen table where she'd left it. "They'll want identification at the hospital, and—"

"It's right there," Sam said, lifting the hand-tooled leather purse.

It was a good thing Mrs. Coley was coming, because Jen's mom, usually so cool and organized, needed someone to take charge.

"Oh, Lord, Samantha, of course it is," Lila said, taking the purse from her. "I'm not that concerned—" She broke off and swallowed loudly. "A broken rib is nothing to worry about. You work around livestock long enough and you're bound to take a tumble or two."

Sam fixed a smile on her lips and nodded, but when she followed Lila toward the blue Mercedes that skidded to a stop in front of the foreman's house, Jen's mom turned and set both hands on Sam's shoulders.

"Honey, I know how much you want to be with Jen and I know it's a lot to ask, but can you please stay here and wait for Jed? It doesn't seem right to just leave him a note."

"I guess," Sam began. Of course she *could*, but she wanted to see Jen.

"He's likely to get mad, first. That's his way when he's worried," Lila warned. "But he'll simmer down after a few minutes. I expect your dad's not much different, so you'll know how to handle him."

Sam nodded. No matter how much she wanted to be with Jen, it was more important that she stay here and "handle" Jed when he got home.

"I could try Linc's cell phone." Mrs. Coley raised her voice so she could be heard through the driver's side window of the Mercedes. "Then he and Jed could just meet us at the hospital."

Sam looked expectantly at Lila, but Jen's mom

didn't consider the possibility for a second.

"I don't think so, Helen. It's a bad idea for me to be anywhere near Linc Slocum right now." Lila's hands closed on the air in a strangling motion. "I'd rather do without Jed than say something to Linc that would get all three of us kicked off this ranch."

Sam understood Lila's anger.

"Don't worry," Sam said. "I'll wait here."

"You're a good friend," Lila said. She gave Sam a strong, one-armed hug, then hurried to the car. She called back, "Help yourself to the muffins, or—"

The crunch of the Mercedes' tires on gravel covered whatever else Lila had said, but Sam didn't mind.

She watched the blue car speed away. For once, she wasn't hungry and she wasn't sure what she was going to do, all alone on Gold Dust Ranch.

Call home, Sam told herself, and then she remembered that Gram had planned to go into town.

Still, she gave it a try. When she dialed the ranch, the phone rang and rang, but no one picked up.

Should she try to find Ryan and tell him what had happened?

Why should she? If he'd ridden along with Jen as he was supposed to, the day might have turned out totally differently.

But Sam reminded herself that Jen had a major crush on Ryan. Tall, stylish, and athletic-looking in a way that reminded her of a polo player, Ryan had smooth coffee-colored hair that Jen just loved. And sometimes, Ryan seemed to like her back.

Sam sighed and gave in. Yes, she should tell him.

Before she went out to search the ranch for Ryan, though, she needed to call Brynna. That way, someone would know where she was and that she needed a ride home.

"I'm not going to get stranded here," Sam muttered, and next she dialed Brynna's office at Willow Springs Wild Horse Center.

The receiver was snatched up on the first ring, but the voice Sam heard wasn't Brynna's.

"Honey, this is Leona speakin' and I'm afraid she's out of the office, settin' things straight for Saturday."

Leona was Brynna's office assistant and she'd worked in the Willow Springs office since it had been built. She knew everything that was going on around the thirty-acre facility, and her expertise freed Brynna to do what she loved most—work with the horses.

"I can flag her down, if that's what you want," Leona added, but something in her voice told Sam that she thought it would be a bad choice to interrupt her stepmother.

"No, that's okay," she said.

"She's been trapped in the office reading applications for people who want to adopt wild horses all morning, and answering the phone that's done nothing but ring with people wondering what color horses we'll have up for adoption, and she just now managed to escape to the outside."

"What color?" Sam repeated, surprised. She would have thought health and temperament were more important.

"Yes, mostly that's what they ask, and their ages, of course. But, honey, what if I take a message and have Brynna call you back?"

Sam heard a swooping sound from outside. Was the big wrought-iron gate swinging open? Was Jed home? Would she be forced to tell him about Jen's accident? And was it true what she'd heard—in ancient times they used to kill messengers who brought bad news?

Of course Jen's dad wouldn't do that, but Jen's mom had said he was likely to be angry when he first heard of his daughter's accident.

"Honey, are you still there?" Leona asked when Sam didn't respond. "Let me go get her if it's important."

"No," Sam said, though it *was* important. "You don't have to do that, but—"

Sam walked to the end of the phone cord, craning her neck to see who was outside. When she didn't see anyone, she finished, "—would you please tell her to pick me up at the Kenworthys' house on her way home?"

"Will do, honey," Leona said.

Once she'd hung up, Sam started outside, but she

hadn't even opened the door when the Kenworthys'
phone rang.

Should she answer the phone? There was practically no chance it was for her. Then again, it could
be. Jen's mother and Ross knew she was here. Not
that Mrs. Kenworthy could be at the hospital yet, but
Ross should be, and whoever it was would give up in
a minute if she didn't answer.

Sam snatched up the phone.

"Hello?" she blurted.

"So glad you picked up, Sam. It's Leona, again."

"Oh, hi."

"Sorry to disappoint you," Leona joked, and for
the millionth time Sam scolded herself for being so
transparent.

"No, it's just—"

Leona didn't give her time to tell about Jen's
accident.

"Thing is, Brynna stuck her head in the office just
after I hung up talking to you and she insisted I tell
you to stay right there at Kenworthys'. Don't move a
muscle, and she'll swing by to get you on her way
home. She *said* to tell you she didn't want to drive all
that distance out of her way and have you gone home
already . . ." Leona's voice lowered to a whisper. "I'm
not sure she's feeling too good, Sam. She's not quite
herself."

Sam's mind darted back to this morning. Despite
her squabble with Dad, Brynna had looked fine.

"Now that I think about it, Brynna might just have something else on her mind." Leona's voice was still conspiratorial but suddenly lighter. "Don't be surprised if she's planned a nice surprise for you all."

"Like what?" Sam asked.

Brynna was big on surprises. She could arrive home with anything from takeout pizza to an abused horse.

"It wouldn't be a surprise if I told, but you'll be the first to hear, if I know anything about your stepmama." Leona was still chuckling when she hung up.

When Sam left the foreman's house, she saw there were no more vehicles parked in front of Linc Slocum's mansion. She shrugged. Whatever she'd heard, it hadn't been a new arrival.

There was no sense walking up there to investigate when Silly was nickering for attention.

"Hey, pretty girl, you have been so patient."

With a twinge of guilt, Sam loosed the palomino's cinch, and slid her hand over the horse. She wasn't hot. Surprisingly, her hair wasn't stiff from sweat, either, though she'd traveled a long way between here and Coffee Creek and she must have been scared during all the commotion.

"I had to go talk with Jen's mom," Sam murmured to the horse, "but I should have come back to you before calling Brynna."

When Silly rubbed her cheek against Sam's, as if forgiving her, it left Sam smiling. She leaned out, grabbed the saddle and blanket together, then slid them toward her chest.

With a grunt, Sam realized Jen's saddle was not only bigger, but much heavier than hers.

"Let me put this up, and you'll be back with your family in just a few minutes," Sam told the horse.

Then Sam staggered toward the barn.

As she approached, she heard something.

Grain pouring from a scoop?

"Hello?" Sam called out, but there was no answer.

She shrugged, hoping she was headed in the right direction. She'd never been inside Gold Dust Ranch's tack room. Arms full, she kept her chin up, staring over the saddle at the same time she tried to watch where she was going.

Wait. This time she had heard something for sure.

Chapter Seven ∽

Shy Boots stood alone in the corner of an open box stall.

"Was that you, pretty baby?" Sam asked over her shoulder as she hurried past to place the saddle on an empty rack in the tack room.

Then she returned to the Appaloosa foal.

With his chocolate-brown body and knee-high front socks above faintly striped hooves, Shy Boots was one of the cutest animals Sam had ever seen.

"But that's a strange little whinny," Sam told the foal, and she wondered if it was the voice with which he'd been born.

The colt and his mother, Hotspot, had been the victims of a botched robbery. They'd been separated when Hotspot escaped with the Phantom. In desperation, the thief had given Shy Boots to a petting zoo, where he'd been fostered for a week by a burro.

To Ryan's astonishment, the owner of the burro had refused to sell her. Since the burro had already begun nursing the colt, the refusal meant Ryan had been forced to wean Shy Boots to a bottle.

According to Jen, Shy Boots had cried day and night for his mothers. Finally, he'd become accustomed to a bottle filled with foal formula, but his voice remained rusty.

Ryan thought Shy Boots had damaged his vocal cords with crying, but listening to the colt now, Sam thought it sounded a little like a donkey's bray.

"Who cares?" Sam asked the colt as he pushed his muzzle into her palm. "At least you ended up with a good home."

She wondered where the thief had ended up. Probably because the big yellow Hummer used in the robbery was such an easily identified vehicle, it was found abandoned in a grocery store parking lot in Darton. The thief had earned nothing for his trouble except a fat file at the Darton police station.

It was probably the thought of the thief, creepy Karl Mannix, that made Sam feel like someone was watching her.

Planting a kiss on Shy Boots' velvety nose, Sam hurried back to the tack room, grabbed a brush, and returned to curry Silly before leading her to the pasture that held the Kenworthy palominos.

Sam brushed and smoothed her hand over Silly's coat. At last it shone bright as a gold coin.

"Now you'll fit right in with the rest of them," Sam told Silly.

Mantilla, Sundance, and Golden Rose were all beautiful animals burnished to show off their Quarter Horse conformation and long, rippling manes. They grazed together in a small enclosure, and Sam was surprised to see that Champ—whose registered name was Golden Champagne—grazed alongside them.

After they'd sold the ranch to Linc Slocum, Jen's parents had quickly accepted the trade he'd proposed to give him Champ in exchange for the deed to the foreman's house. Even if they'd known what a poor horseman the millionaire was, they couldn't have refused the bargain.

Linc's kindness in letting Champ graze with his family was totally out of character.

Sam released Silly among the other golden horses, but she couldn't enjoy their beauty. She was too worried about Jen.

What if a broken rib hadn't been Jen's only injury?

What if she'd suffered damage to an internal organ? Her liver could have been injured, or her spleen, or even her heart.

All over again, the bony power of the bull's head

battering Jen swam before Sam's eyes. And then, she had a totally selfish thought.

How would she get through her first week of school alone?

Jen couldn't be back by then, could she? Broken arms and legs could be protected in casts, but what about broken ribs? Sam thought of moving down the crowded halls of school and winced for Jen. Especially during the first week, people bumped into you like crazy. No way could Jen take that.

But neither can I, Sam thought.

She tried to tell herself it wouldn't be like last year, when she hadn't known *any*one. Still, she could number off the people she considered friends on one hand—only Jen and Jake really counted.

At least Jake would be back in time for the beginning of school. Yes, he was a senior, and sure, he was so standoffish at school it made her crazy. But Jake had proven more than once that he was there if she needed him.

There was his friend Darrell, too. A year younger than Jake, Darrell was living down a reputation as a bad boy—which he really wasn't. Sam considered Rjay, the editor of the school paper, a buddy, too. Was it weird that she could come up with more guys than girls when she tried to list her friends? Because when it came to girlfriends, Jen was about it.

Just like in San Francisco, Sam thought with a sigh. *It's not that I'm unfriendly,* Sam told herself. *I'm just not the sort of person who hangs around in big groups.*

In San Francisco, her only close friend had been Pamela O'Malley. For the first time in months, she missed Pam. In San Francisco, they'd played on the same basketball team, had the same classes, and had eaten lunch together across the same table each day. Sam and Pam. Everyone knew they were best friends, and they'd promised to stay close, even when Sam had moved back home.

But it hadn't worked out that way. After their first phone call, conversations grew awkward. They knew different people and did different things. Not that they hadn't tried to stay in touch. Last summer, Pam had been planning to visit River Bend Ranch, but her mother, a cultural anthropologist, had earned a grant to go to Japan.

Sam couldn't blame Pam when she had decided to go along.

"Gorgeous, aren't they?"

Sam's gasp burned her throat.

"You . . . startled me," Sam said.

She'd recognized Ryan's silky British accent immediately and she'd halfway expected to hear it, but not right at her elbow.

Ryan's teasing smile said he knew it.

"Sorry. I was graining Sky Ranger when I heard you," he said.

Uh-huh. She *had* heard grain rushing out of a scoop, and then she'd gone on to have a whole kissy conversation with Shy Boots. But she wouldn't give Ryan the satisfaction of knowing he'd scared her, especially when there were more important things on her mind.

"Jen's hurt," she blurted.

"No," he said with slow disbelief. For a second, he looked as worried as Sam felt, but then he exhaled loudly. "Something minor, I suppose, and that's why you're here doing her chores? I didn't see you as the trespassing sort."

"There was an accident," Sam told him.

"She must be all right, or you wouldn't be here," he said.

At that, Sam felt a small spurt of pleasure. Ryan understood she wouldn't desert Jen if she needed help.

Once she'd finished explaining what had happened, Ryan asked, "Do you think she'd want to see me?"

This was a side of Ryan that Sam could like. Uncertainty made him seem like a nicer person.

"Sure, she'd like to see you," Sam said.

"Even if she's all banged up and dirty?" Ryan asked.

Sam sighed. "I'm pretty sure that's not the first thing on her mind right now. Broken bones kind of hurt."

"I daresay," Ryan allowed. Then he patted at a pocket, probably looking for his car keys. "Would you like to ride along, now that you've taken care of her horse?"

"I really would," Sam said, "but I promised Jen's mom that I'd stay and tell Jed what happened."

Ryan gave an impatient shrug. "Leave him a note."

"I promised to stay and explain," Sam said.

"I guess there's no sense offering you a ride home, then, either," Ryan said, fishing car keys from his pocket.

Sam shook her head. Though the day was slipping away, she had to do what she'd promised Lila.

She stared after Ryan and tried to be happy for Jen. Ryan liked her enough to drive into Darton to check on her. That satisfaction would have to do, because Sam had a feeling that she could talk all day and Ryan still wouldn't understand what it meant to give your word.

Some days Sam thought her best friend's dad had sad-looking eyes. This wasn't one of those days. Right now, Jed Kenworthy's eyes glared with fury.

"Ross let her get gored?"

"No, the bull didn't have horns—"

"And Lila? Where's she?"

"At the hospital. Mrs. Coley drove her. They thought about calling Linc's cell phone but, uh, Mrs. Kenworthy said she wasn't sure she should be around Linc. I mean—"

"I know what you mean," Jed snapped. "What I don't know is why Ross wasn't the one down in that pen instead of Jennifer."

As soon as he'd said the words, a flash of guilt crossed Jed's face. His daughter had worked beside him, branding cattle, mucking out irrigation ditches, roping steers out of heavy brush, and more. Now, he seemed to be wondering if all that had been a mistake.

"We shoulda kept her home where she belonged," Jed muttered. "I knew it, but she would go to town, and we didn't stand up to her."

Could she have heard him right? Sam wondered.

Jed's comment seemed to be about Jen going to school, not into a corral of wild bulls.

"Snorty." Disgust at how he'd misjudged the bull filled Jed's voice. "All I told her was that the bull from Fishbait Springs was snorty."

Jed's hands covered his face, and Sam swallowed hard. It was scary to see an adult in such despair.

As Sam's mind raced to think of what she could say or do, she heard Jed whisper, "That child is home for good."

Sam didn't like the sound of that.

"What if you called the hospital?" Sam urged. "I bet they'd know something by now. Maybe it wasn't as bad as it looked."

What a stupid thing to say, Sam thought. She'd left Jed wondering how bad it *had* looked. Sam shrank back into her own raised shoulders, wishing she could vanish.

Jed didn't seem to hear.

He just nodded slowly and said, "Good idea." But then his head cocked to one side and his eyes narrowed, listening to the vehicle approaching the ranch gates.

Relief poured over Sam at the sight of Dad's truck.

"It's Ross! He'll tell us how Jen is!" Sam was excited until she turned toward Jed.

"If that cowboy knows what's good for him, he'll be tellin' me more than that. He never shoulda let this happen."

Inside the ranch gates, Ross slowed the gray truck to get a better look at the Shetland ponies running alongside the white fence.

Keep driving. Turn around and go home!

Although she knew it was hopeless, Sam tried to send Ross a message to escape. Jed wanted someone to blame, and when Ross emerged from the truck smiling, Sam knew it was the worst thing he could have done.

"What happened to my little girl?" Jed growled.

Ross stopped. "Sh-she's okay," he managed to say, but his ruddy face drained to the color of milk, and Sam saw a scar across his top lip that she'd never noticed before.

"She'd better be okay," Jed said. "You're the experienced cowhand. How could you let this happen?"

Should she jump between these two adults and

interrupt? She'd been there. She'd seen the attack. She knew the same thing might have happened if Jed had been there instead of Ross.

It was the way Ross looked that finally decided her. Earlier today she'd thought he looked like a bear. He still did, like a dancing bear on a chain. He look trapped, a big strong creature who didn't know what he was supposed to do. With downcast eyes, he shambled from side to side.

"Speak up!" Jed shouted when Ross stayed quiet.

Sam had seen this happen before, but for the first time she knew why Ross wet his lips, but then shook his head and studied the dirt again.

Ross wasn't just shy. He didn't speak up for fear he'd start stuttering and not be able to stop. That's what had happened out by the cattle pens. The harder he tried to force past the stutter, the worse it had gotten.

"Mr. Kenworthy," Sam protested. "We were doing exactly what Jen said you wanted us to do. Ross was right there in the pen standing next to her, but the bull just picked Jen to chase."

Jed didn't look away from Ross.

"Right beside her? And what did you do? What did *you*"—Jed gestured toward Ross's height and wide shoulders—"do to stop the bull from goin' after my little girl?"

"N-not—"

"He hit it with his hat, then he shoved it and

punched it and—" Sam drew a breath before she went on.

"Let him tell it." Jed leaned forward and cupped a hand to his ear. "What did you do while a ton of wild-range bull charged down on my baby?"

Ross still didn't look up, but Sam understood the two words he fought to pronounce.

"He said 'not enough,'" Sam blurted.

"You got that right," Jed said. Then, maybe because his anger had spent itself or maybe because he realized he wasn't being fair, Jed's hand dismissed Ross. "Just get outta here."

But Jed was the one who moved first, walking stiffly toward the house.

Sam was pretty sure he'd call the hospital now, just as he would have if Ross hadn't come here, if Ross hadn't been nice enough to stop for her.

Sam was thinking the bull had wanted to blame someone for taking him from the freedom of the range and confining him in a little corral. Jed wanted to blame someone for Jen's accident.

It was almost the same, but Sam couldn't assemble the words to explain what she was thinking to Ross and it probably wouldn't have helped anyway.

When Sam looked at the big cowboy, Ross closed his eyes. When they reopened, Ross's eyes met hers with a pained expression. Then he nodded toward the truck.

"I can't. I told Brynna I'd wait here until she

picked me up," Sam said. "I'd rather go with you."
She rushed on when Ross looked even more downcast.
"But I promised."

Ross lumbered back toward the truck.

Dad will understand, she wanted to shout after him.
You won't get in trouble.
He'll believe me. . . .

Sam longed to promise Ross all those things, but
she wasn't sure she was right.

Chapter Eight ❧

"Sent home by a vet, can you believe that?" Brynna said as Sam got into her white BLM truck. "Not even a human doctor, but a *vet*, sent me home from work to get some rest," Brynna mused as they drove away from Gold Dust Ranch.

Sam was glad to escape.

More than anything, she'd wanted to go after Jed and make him understand that Jen's injury still would have happened if he'd been there. Ross wasn't to blame, but Sam was afraid her insistence would only make Jed angrier. So, she'd wandered from pasture to corral to box stall, trying to draw comfort from the sounds of healthy horses grinding grass, swishing tails, snorting, and stamping, while she waited for Brynna to arrive.

Only once had her trance been interrupted. The door on the foreman's house had opened. Without coming outside, Jed had shouted, "One broke rib is all." Then the door had slammed closed like an exclamation mark.

Now, settling into Brynna's truck and double-checking her seat belt, Sam wasn't sure how to tell Brynna all that had happened.

First Jen's accident, Sam thought, and then Jed's unfair attack on Ross, but just as she opened her mouth to begin, Brynna turned toward her with a half smile.

"I'd be really mad at Dr. Scott if I hadn't been so eager to tell you something."

"Wait," Sam said. What was she thinking? Jen was fine, uncomfortable maybe, in the Darton hospital, but she was under the best of care. And Ross, sad and hurt as he must be, was probably fine, too. Sam imagined him home at River Bend, checking Tank's feet and caring for the big Quarter Horse as he always did when he had a moment of leisure. But Brynna had just said she'd been sent home from work to rest!

"What happened? What's wrong with you?"

"I'm fine," Brynna said. She reached over to tug loose one of Sam's hands.

If she hadn't, Sam might not even have realized her arms had crossed tightly over her middle. Brynna placed Sam's hand on the seat between them and gave it a pat.

"I was on the catwalk above the loading chutes—"

Sam pictured the metal fences that formed the passages through which the wild horses moved before being loaded into the trailers that would carry them to their new homes. Eight or ten feet in the air, above them, there were catwalks—places from which to supervise the safety of the horses.

"—looking from up above to make sure I hadn't missed anything—uneven footing or a bolt sticking out the horses could cut themselves on—"

"You didn't fall, did you?" Sam asked.

"No—well, not *off*," she amended. "I just got a little dizzy as I was climbing down and missed a couple steps. Don't worry, this little buckaroo is pretty well protected," Brynna said, patting her rounded blouse.

"And Dr. Scott was there," Sam prodded.

Sam was amazed. Dr. Scott was usually kind of laid back, so he must have been worried. Sam didn't say that, though. Brynna knew the young vet well enough to realize his concern. That's probably why she'd done what he'd advised.

At least, that's what Sam was thinking until Brynna turned right out of Gold Dust's driveway, instead of left.

"I have something to show you." Brynna answered Sam's question before she asked it.

"Are we going back to Willow Springs?" Sam asked.

"Yes," Brynna said, nodding, "but we're not driving past my office. My watchdog Dr. Scott might be there updating some of the data we have on the horses, and even though he's not my doctor, I don't want him barking at me."

A faint smile played over Brynna's lips as she drove, and finally Sam had to end the suspense.

"You've picked out a new horse, haven't you? For HARP?"

Brynna shook her head and corrected Sam. "For Wyatt." She paused for only a second before launching into a description. "Oh, Sam, you'll love him. He's a funny little horse—independent as a cat, but he was herd stallion of a small band at Good Thunder Meadows and he likes to think for himself. You'll find out tomorrow when you try to move him from one corral to another. He's not scared or stubborn, he just does what he likes, when he likes."

While Brynna drove, Sam pictured the stallion from Good Thunder Meadows standing face-to-face with Dad and smiled. People said she and Dad were equally stubborn and they got along most of the time, so why wouldn't it work with a horse?

"So, you think he should be named Thunder?"

"Whatever your dad wants," Brynna said. "In my experience, naming your horse is part of the bonding process."

Sam's image of Dad and the horse faded under the sensible realization that Dad was never eager to take on another mouth to feed. And he expected every creature on the ranch to earn its keep.

How long would it take to gentle this horse to saddle?

She didn't want to take the sunshine from Brynna's face, but she wasn't sure Dad would accept the new horse and spend the time it took to train him, even if he was a gift.

"If you're wondering how I'll get Wyatt to take him, you'll just have to trust the horse," Brynna said. "He's been at Willow Springs for over a month, but I only really saw him a few days ago and the minute I did, I knew he'd be perfect for Wyatt. He's so smart you can see it in his eyes, figuring things out rather than just bolting in panic. He's been in captivity for nearly a year, too, so he tolerates people. Although," Brynna said, chuckling, "I can't say he respects them."

"Are you sure that's what Dad wants?" Sam asked. Dad's favorite horse Banjo had seemed to read Dad's mind, not think for himself.

But Brynna looked determined.

"Even if Wyatt doesn't bond with him right away, one of us is going to repay that animal for what's been taken away from him."

"What happened?" Sam asked.

Brynna made a hard right turn off the asphalt and

followed the dirt road that led up to Thread the Needle.

"It was a mistake, nothing malicious," Brynna assured her, "but someone should have questioned the decision to remove the herd from Good Thunder Meadows. It's far north, almost to the Oregon border, and it's known for harsh weather. His little band of five had tolerated it by moving around, in and out of the meadows, up and down the hillsides, following food and water for generations.

"But BLM determined that drought had made the territory uninhabitable, and the horses were brought in."

Brynna sighed, and Sam wondered why Brynna was so upset by this small gather. Although they'd both rather see the wild horses run free, the BLM's adoption program was a compromise made with cattlemen a long time ago—when Gram had been a newly married bride.

"Is something about this band special?" Sam asked, knowing Brynna would understand.

"One of the adopters of a grulla mare and foal was interested in Spanish Mustangs and thought those two had the look and that wonderful floating gait—like a Paso Fino." Brynna glanced over at Sam to verify she knew what she was talking about, and Sam nodded, even though she wasn't positive.

They'd reached the single-lane portion of the road that freaked Sam out every time she looked over the edge. She tried not to do it. But some irresistible force seemed to draw Sam's eyes, making her look. Willow Springs looked like a toy ranch down below, with sunlight glinting off the roofs.

"When she had them tested," Brynna went on, "the mare and foal turned out to be almost pure Spanish."

Sam thought of conquistadors and guitar music, of exotic horses mincing down a gangplank from Christopher Columbus's ship.

"And they've been living up in that meadow all this time?" Sam asked. She'd learned about this in biology. Specialized animals developed on islands or in places where they couldn't easily leave and intermingle with other species. "But the herd just dwindled down to six?"

Brynna nodded. "The stallion, a yearling colt, two older mares, and their foals. My guess is that the herd size shrank and grew according to range conditions, just like most horse herds," Brynna said. "But it doesn't matter now."

"Sure it does! Maybe they were about to die out and now those bloodlines can be preserved," Sam insisted.

"If someone had noticed in time, maybe," Brynna said. "But the stallion—this pretty boy I'm about to show you—and his yearling colt were gelded. Neither of them will be siring any pure Spanish offspring. One of the mares didn't survive being trucked from Nevada to the adoption facility in California, and I haven't been able to track down her foal."

Driving slowly, Brynna took a less traveled path that spurred off from the main road to Willow Springs.

"We'll take a trail that goes behind the corrals. We're not moving the older stallions and geldings up for viewing until tomorrow, so we'll have a little privacy."

Even though they weren't far away, just about the height of a single-story house, Brynna took a pair of binoculars from their leather case and looped the strap over Sam's neck.

"He's in with a nice group of horses," Brynna said.

Through the dust settling around them, Sam could make out a bright bay, a buckskin, and two light-colored horses, maybe grays.

"I don't think you'll have any trouble picking him out. He has a certain attitude," Brynna said. "But I want you to get a good, close look at him so you can tell me if you think he's right for your dad."

The Spanish Mustang had attitude, all right. At the sight of humans, he broke away from the other horses and headed toward them.

Glossy as the inside of a seashell, his coat was ivory with blue-gray markings that flashed with a metallic gleam, but it wasn't his color that made him stand out.

A little taller than Ace, smooth-muscled, and strong, the horse was definitely showing off. He moved with a fluid gait that made the sweeps of blue roan behind each shoulder look like wings.

"He looks like he could fly," Sam gasped.

"Like I said, that's part of what tipped off the adopters to the herd's heritage," Brynna said. "Now, imagine what a smooth ride he'd give Wyatt as he crosses the range."

Sam nodded, but her memory had veered in another direction.

"Have you ever talked with Dallas about that pacing white stallion that's in all kinds of myths? He must look like this. But his markings —"

"—are great?" Brynna finished for her. "I know. The shapes look just like folded wings, don't they, even tapering toward the tips with that feathery edge?"

Sam raised the binoculars to her eyes and studied the horse as he turned. "And they look like they're almost identical on both sides of his body," Sam said.

"They are."

Sam could tell from the sound of her stepmother's voice that Brynna was smiling, but she couldn't take her eyes away from the mustang to be sure.

Even though the truck's windows were open, Sam heard no grate of hooves on sand as the gelding stopped near the hay rack. Head lifted, he turned intelligent brown eyes on them.

"He's trying to be patient with us," Brynna joked, "but it's a strain. I mean, what good are we if we're not feeding him?"

Sam laughed when the mustang shook his flaxen mane. She couldn't tell if it was silver or gold, but its fine texture reminded her of tinsel.

"He's going to give us thirty seconds more, and then time's up," Brynna said as the gelding wheeled away and smoothly crossed the corral, brushing back the buckskin that had moved between him and the gate.

"He just thought of one other thing we're good for," Sam said. "Opening the gate."

As the horse reached the opposite end of the corral, once more he went from a breathtaking motion to a complete stop as quietly as a bird landing on a branch. Then he waited.

"He's used to being the boss," Sam said. "Dad would have to earn his respect."

"He wouldn't be a push-button horse, that's for sure," Brynna agreed. "But he's trainable. With the right bribe, you can touch him now."

"What's the right bribe?" Sam asked.

"He's pretty fond of your gram's oatmeal cookies," Brynna admitted. "But he spits out the raisins, and even though he'll literally eat out of your hand, he's not sweet and docile. It's more like he's doing you a favor, with some future payoff in mind."

"I know just what you're talking about," Sam said. "That's how Ace was when I first got him."

"So, what do you think?" Brynna asked as Sam lowered the binoculars.

Sam could hardly wait to take the mustang home. "I think you've picked a winner."

"Uh-oh," Brynna said, and it only took Sam a few seconds to realize her stepmother wasn't responding to what Sam had said about the Spanish Mustang.

Dr. Glen Scott stood near a Willow Springs corral about half a mile away, but his hand shaded his eyes as he gazed upward.

"Back in the truck! Hurry!" Brynna yelped, then she added, "I don't like acting like a guilty kid, but I'm not going to have another 'what's-good-for-my-health' conversation, either."

Sam giggled as they made their getaway. When she looked back at the Spanish Mustang, his mouth was wide open, showing his pink tongue and white teeth.

Was he yawning? Or laughing?

Chapter Nine ❧

As they started home, Brynna grumbled.

"It's a good thing I'm organized for this adoption day. Not only did I miss part of this afternoon, but I have to take two days of annual leave—one for tomorrow and another on Saturday."

"Why? You haven't taken a day off—except for your honeymoon—since I've known you," Sam said.

"I hope that makes me a good role model," Brynna said, shooting a side glance Sam's way.

"Sure," Sam said, shrugging. "But I don't miss much school."

Suddenly, though, she considered the possibility. What if she faked a sore throat or the flu, so she wouldn't have to start school without Jen?

No way, her conscience insisted.

While Sam tried to convince her guilty conscience that it would be a once-in-a-lifetime fib, Brynna was explaining that as a BLM employee who wanted to adopt a wild horse she had to be counseled by her superior.

"That means a trip into Reno tomorrow to talk with Rex," Brynna said. "And, although he says he doesn't mind, it means he has to work overtime—driving out here on Saturday to direct the adoption day."

Rex Black was Brynna's boss, and though Sam had never met him, she'd heard his name many times.

"Why do you have to go by special rules?" Sam asked. "Isn't that, like, discrimination?"

Brynna took one hand from the steering wheel and made a wavering motion. "Depends on how you look at it," she said. "What if someone accused me of spotting the best horse and adopting him before anyone else had a chance? And someone might think I could pull something shady if I were in charge of adoptions on the day I wanted to bid on a horse of my own. But it doesn't really matter. I've got things under control. Besides, with you and Jen on the scene—"

"But no," Sam interrupted.

"No?" Brynna asked.

Sam's mind spun. She'd been so excited over the Spanish Mustang, she still hadn't told Brynna what had happened to Jen and how she'd ended up stranded at Gold Dust Ranch.

"I mean, I'll help, of course," Sam said. "But this morning—"

All at once, it was hard to talk past the lump in her throat.

You expected to see charging bulls plowing into people and lifting them off their feet in a movie, but not in real life.

"Sam?" Brynna frowned and pushed back a strand of reddish hair that had escaped from her French braid. "You're scaring me."

"When we were out taking care of those Gold Dust Ranch bulls this morning, there was an accident."

"Oh no," Brynna said. She glanced into her rearview mirror, spotted a car behind them, and pulled over onto the shoulder of the road to let it zip past. "Tell me what happened."

"Jen got charged by a bull and it broke one of her ribs."

"Did she fall while it was after her and—"

"No, it got her down and was like goring her, but it had no horns," Sam said.

"Oh no," Brynna said again. "But you girls weren't alone?" It was more of a demand than a question.

"No, Dad had to take some hay to Caleb Sawyer, so he sent Ross with us, but the bull just picked Jen to go after. It didn't make any sense. She didn't do anything wrong."

"Ross was with you," Brynna repeated, as if that should have made a difference.

Sam found herself rushing to defend Ross again. "He did all he could, but the bull was just . . ." Sam pictured the animal ramming Jen's side. "Fixated."

Brynna drew a deep breath and shook her head.

"It wasn't Ross's fault!" Sam insisted.

"Okay," Brynna said in a soothing tone. "I didn't mean to imply that it was."

"You didn't. I'm sorry. It's Jed. He thinks Ross is totally to blame. I told him he was wrong, but he wanted Ross to explain, and when he tried . . ."

Sam closed her lips. If Ross wanted everyone to know about his disability, they would know. He was trying to keep it to himself. It wasn't her secret to tell.

"Did Jed yell at him?" Brynna asked.

"Oh yeah."

"And Ross stuttered?"

In the quiet moment, a meadowlark's liquid song rose from the tall roadside grass and blew in the open truck window.

Sam felt relieved. Maybe Brynna could help make things better.

"You know about that?" Sam asked.

"Wyatt told me," Brynna said, "and though I don't feel any compulsion to talk with Ross about it, I don't think it should be a big dark mystery, either. Still, that's for him to decide." Then Brynna added, "It's how he lost his last job."

How weird, Sam thought. She'd never thought of Ross having another job.

"Why would it matter how a cowboy talks?"

"Before he came to River Bend he wasn't a cowboy. He was doing construction work in Montana, and I guess—" Brynna pursed her lips in concentration. "I hope I have this right, but I think a guy accidentally shot himself with a nail gun."

Sam winced. The men working on building the barn after the fire had used nail guns, and they'd fired with lots of force.

"Ross was right beside this guy," Brynna went on, "but when he tried to call for help, he had trouble talking and the foreman couldn't understand him."

How awful, Sam thought, like a silent scream in the worst of nightmares. Only it had been real.

"He stutters when he's scared?" Sam asked.

"When he's under pressure, he told your dad," Brynna said, "so, I guess even though Ross did everything else right—immobilizing the nail and getting the guy down safely from the roof they were working on—that wasn't enough for the foreman. He called Ross names and—" Brynna hesitated. "He said some pretty unkind things."

Being able to speak without stuttering wouldn't have changed anything today, Sam thought.

"It really wasn't him. I think maybe the bull had some kind of vision problem," Sam said.

"Your dad will believe you," Brynna assured her.

"So will Jed after he simmers down. I mean, think of it logically. Jen's your best friend in the world. You'd be blaming Ross with every breath in your body if he deserved it."

"Yep," Sam said, and just as she was thinking how great Brynna was at putting things into perspective, her stepmother yawned.

Taking one hand from the steering wheel, Brynna covered her mouth, then they both turned at the sound of a car slowing on the highway.

"It's Gram!" Sam said.

The yellow Buick swerved. Since there was no other traffic on the road, Gram stopped and let her car idle beside the BLM truck.

"Are you two all right?" Gram shouted.

"Fine," Brynna said in a consoling voice. Then she joked, "You know how I always talk with my hands? Well, I decided I could either drive or talk, but not both. So we stopped for a second."

Gram didn't look convinced, but she didn't ask what was so important that they had to talk about it here at the roadside.

"You're not with Ross," Gram pointed out.

"There was an accident." Sam spoke past Brynna and aimed her words at Gram. "Ross had to take Jen to the hospital in Darton. Jen was charged by a bull and she broke a rib."

Gram tsked her tongue. "I remember my daddy whipping off his shirt and using it to distract a bull from one of us kids, once."

Sam thought of the way she'd flapped Jen's sweatshirt at the bull. Maybe she'd been on the right track, but her matador trick hadn't worked.

"I tried that," Sam said, hoping Gram would praise her good sense. But she didn't.

"My lands," Gram said, then added, "Well, I guess Trudy'll have to wait one more day to get her flies sprayed."

Sam wondered if her head actually snapped back in surprise at Gram's lack of sympathy. Jen had a broken rib. She could have been killed, but all Gram could think about was Mrs. Allen's flies!

"We'll see you at home," Brynna said, and then, as Gram raised a hand in farewell and drove on, she added to Sam, "I don't know how they do it—your dad and Gram."

"Do what?" Sam snapped. "Think it's a bigger deal that Mrs. Allen has flies than my best friend is in the hospital?"

Brynna shifted uncomfortably, drew her seat belt back on, then clicked it into place. "There wouldn't be any animals or any ranch if they didn't put them first. It's been that way for generations and we both need to remember that. And be grateful."

"I guess," Sam said, then sighed, because she knew Gram really did care, even if it hadn't sounded like it.

For some reason, then, Sam's mind veered back to the horses.

"About the mustangs from Good Thunder

Meadows . . ." She paused as Brynna smiled and nodded. "The grulla mare and her foal weren't lost, and though it would have been cool to have those bloodlines in Nevada's wild horses, at least River Bend will have its own Spanish Mustang."

"True," Brynna said. "Assuming I'm high bidder on him."

"And assuming Strawberry will share her throne," Sam added.

Brynna laughed. "That mare has been queen of the saddle horse pasture since I moved in."

"Me too," Sam said.

As they pulled back on the highway, headed for home, Sam couldn't help feeling glad that Brynna was her stepmother.

Because even though she was weary and worried, when Brynna thought about horses, she smiled as if she were floating on a cloud.

Chapter Ten ⟨⟩

$\mathcal{A}$ce's neigh reached Sam even before the truck had crossed the bridge over the La Charla River.

The Spanish Mustang might be smart, but Ace was brilliant. How could he know that she was riding home with Brynna when she'd left here with Ross?

Love for the little bay horse poured over Sam's heart, washing away the sting of Jen's pain and Jed's anger.

Glinting red gold in the late summer sundown, Ace rushed along the fence. Wind tossed his black forelock so she could see the white star between his eyes. If she could just wrap her arms around Ace's neck and breathe his grassy sweetness, everything would be okay.

"Can I get out here?" Sam asked.

Brynna braked to an instant stop.

"Go," she said, and Sam did, then ran to the fence surrounding the ten-acre pasture.

Ace stood waiting, head slung over the top rail. He stretched his nose toward her. Then he nudged his face against her chest, but Sam only got in a single hug, a few seconds with her cheek pressed to his coarse black mane, before the gelding backed away, snorting.

"Does this mean you want to go for a ride instead of hugging?" she asked.

Ace looked over her shoulder and down the gravel road that led to the bridge, to the cottonwoods fringing the river.

"There might be time tonight, if you don't mind a tagalong," Sam told him. "I already promised Tempest that I'd work with her."

Ace snapped his head to face her and his ears pricked forward.

"Okay, we'll work it out," she told him, and Ace walked away, out of reach, returning to the other horses in the pasture.

Sam jogged to catch up with Brynna. Her stepmother had stopped next to Dad's new gray truck.

Dad's old truck was missing, though he stood across the ranch yard patting Strawberry's shoulder and releasing her hoof as if he'd just been squatting to examine it. Gram stood nearby, and they were talking.

When Sam reached the white truck, the driver's side door was open and Brynna still sat inside.

"Ross must have already gone to help Mrs. Allen," Sam said. She expected Brynna to say something like, *If neighbors didn't help neighbors, no one could have settled out here,* but Brynna didn't say anything.

Flushed pink, Brynna sat fanning herself with her hand.

"Carrying this little one around is like having my own private heater," Brynna muttered. "I can't say I need that right now."

Sam gave Brynna a sympathetic smile. She was about to offer to take care of Penny, Brynna's mare, when the copper mustang neighed. Brynna's weariness vanished and her smile returned.

"Let's go see what your dad's doing," Brynna said, slipping down from the truck.

Whether it was Ace's greeting or the prospect of bringing home a new horse, Sam felt her mood soar.

"What's happening?" Sam asked, bouncing up to give Dad a hug.

He gave her a quick pat on the back and then took off his hat and brushed it free of dust as he talked.

"Seems like you came to the right place to ask," Dad said. "Don't know how I got to be secretary for this whole danged family, but Jed called."

"He did?"

"Don't need to be worried," Dad told her. "He gave me an earful about Ross and Jen." Dad paused, and though his eyes shifted to her face with a glint of sympathy, he didn't ask her about the accident. "Next, Mr. Blair called to confirm you were meetin' with the Journalism class tomorrow night."

What? Sam thought. Confirm? But that would mean it was something she already knew about.

"Somethin' about a welcome back project," Dad added.

Sam swallowed hard, thinking of the stack of school mail Gram had been urging her to go through. With a sickly feeling, she wondered if she should have done that days ago.

"And you," Dad said, brushing a strand of auburn hair back from Brynna's sweaty forehead, "missed your doctor's appointment."

"Oh!" Brynna gasped. "Did you go? Were you waiting for me?" She pressed her hands to her cheeks and shook her head. "I forgot!"

"Settle down, B.," Dad said, looking a little worried.

"But you drove all the way in and then you were waiting—"

"Not for long," Dad said. "Not much point to me and the doctor gettin' together without you."

Sam could tell Dad was joking, but Brynna's eyes had filled with tears.

"What's wrong with my brain?" she demanded. "I'm pregnant, not simpleminded. I do not forget appointments!"

"Oh, now," Gram began, but Brynna didn't seem to hear her.

"What kind of mother am I going to be? Will I leave my baby in a car seat and go into Clara's for lunch? Will I leave my daughter waiting in the dark after soccer practice? Or forget my son's appointment to be fitted for his tuxedo for the prom?"

Sam held in her giggle because Brynna was so obviously distressed, but Gram laughed out loud, caught Brynna in a hug, and wouldn't let her struggle loose.

"You've got plenty of time to practice being a good mother," Gram insisted. "Missing one appointment isn't worth a minute's worry when you have your hands full with this adoption day, and picking up Samantha."

Wait! Was this turning into her fault?

"Hey," Sam began, but the stare Gram shot her over Brynna's shoulder told Sam to hush. Gram didn't really blame her. She was just offering Brynna excuses.

"Thanks," Brynna said as Gram finally released her and Dad pulled her into a safe place under his arm.

Gram gave a satisfied nod.

"Now, as soon as you've had yourself a little rest while I make dinner, I'm going to need your help," Gram said, and Sam wondered why that seemed to make Brynna perk up.

"Of course," Brynna said. "What do you need?"

"*We* need to figure out what kind of radios to install in the truck. Wyatt and I have talked for years about doing it. Lands, we could have saved endless trouble if we'd had some way to communicate from the range to the home ranch," Gram said.

"Can we afford them?" Brynna asked.

"We'll have to," Gram said.

"Now that Sweetheart's taking her meals elsewhere," Dad said, referring to the pinto mare they'd donated to a riding therapy program, "we can use her feed money for a few extras."

Not if we're getting a new horse, Sam thought. And the Spanish Mustang was a strong, energetic ten-year-old. He'd probably eat even more.

Brynna met Sam's eyes. She must be thinking the same thing, but she just sniffed loudly as if tears might be threatening again.

"We can't afford not to buy them," Gram said. "This accident of Jen's could have happened to one of us just as easily. And though you and Ross handled things just fine," Gram said when Sam started to protest, "we can't count on luck to keep us safe."

"Luck?" Sam couldn't help blurting the word.

She couldn't think of one lucky thing about Jen's accident. Luck would have been if the bull had missed Jen and she'd had time to scramble over the corral fence to safety.

"Luck," Dad repeated firmly. "What if the bull had

taken after Ross? How would you girls have moved him to the truck and driven him to the hospital?"

Chills rained down Sam's arms.

"I didn't think of that," she admitted. Even working together, she and Jen could have hurt Ross far worse trying to move him. Then, because she was imagining Ross's pain, she asked, "Was he okay?"

"Sure he is. We didn't talk," Dad said, and Sam guessed Ross and Dad had just gone with an earlier plan to swap vehicles—without conversation. "But he's a tough cowboy, Sam."

"But you didn't see his face," Sam began.

"Don't worry about him," Dad said. "Worry about gettin' inside to call Mr. Blair back. Doesn't seem right, you gettin' into trouble with your teacher and school hasn't even started yet."

"Yes, sir," Sam said. She tried to be extra polite, because Dad had a point.

"I've got to get dinner started, so I'll go along in with you," Gram said, and Sam walked with her in companionable silence until Gram added, "If you'd read that back-to-school information I put on your desk up in your bedroom, I suspect you might not have anything to worry about."

"I'm not worried," Sam protested.

"Probably wouldn't hurt to read over the information about gym clothes and lockers, either."

"I'm not ready for summer to be over!"

"No complaining when you've had the entire

summer off," Gram said.

Off? Sam thought of the weeding, shoveling, scrubbing, and brushing that had hardened her muscles and scuffed her knuckles all summer long, but just then the phone rang. Rather than get herself into trouble, she hurried ahead to answer it.

It must be Jen. It seemed like she'd been waiting all day for news of her best friend, so she grabbed the receiver before Gram could beat her to it.

"Hope you've had a restful summer, Forster, because I'm expecting you to hit the ground running." Mr. Blair always sounded more like a coach than a teacher.

"My gram and I were just talking about that," Sam said.

She wasn't exactly sure what he meant, but she was pretty sure he'd said the same thing last year, on the first day of class. Now, Sam guessed he was going to keep her busy because she was photo editor for the school newspaper.

The thought was exciting, but she felt a bit queasy. Should she have been preparing all summer for her new job?

"On the night before school starts, there'll be what Mrs. Santos is calling an 'event,'" Mr. Blair said. "All the major clubs—and she's counting newspaper and yearbook in that category—" Mr. Blair didn't sound as if he agreed with the classification, but she guessed he'd go along with the principal's decision.

Sam knew from experience that Mrs. Santos was a tough person to turn down. "—are supposed to do something on the last night of summer to make everyone feel eager to return the next morning."

"Is that possible?" Sam joked.

"I'm counting on you to think of something warm and fuzzy, Forster, because Rjay and I aren't the type," Mr. Blair said.

And I am? Sam wanted to ask.

But this was her first semester as an editor. And she'd won the position over Rachel Slocum. Rachel had vowed that meant the end of her days in Journalism, but Sam wasn't convinced. Rachel loved to get the scoop on hot news that she could translate into gossip. And if Rachel was around, she'd be absolutely delighted to step in and take the job if Sam messed up.

So Sam tried to be cooperative.

"Do we know what the other clubs are doing?" she asked.

"Math Club has already snapped up food duty. They're doing a free hot dog barbecue out in the quad. The Spirit Squad is putting up decorations. The Ecology Club is in charge of music and they've already been on campus wiring up speakers and testing their sound system."

"Why does it sound like they got first choice?" Sam asked, but as soon as the words had passed her lips, she regretted it.

"Because I didn't get calls back from you slacker Journalism kids!" Mr. Blair almost shouted. "Now we're up against a deadline. Tomorrow's Friday. School starts next Thursday. Tomorrow we're meeting to decide what to do for entertainment."

"Entertainment?" Sam yelped.

"Put on your thinking cap, Forster," Mr. Blair ordered, "and I'll expect to see your happy face tomorrow morning at eight A.M. in the J room."

Sam hung up the phone and stared at it. She didn't know she'd made a sound until Gram said, "I rarely hear you moan, Samantha."

Gram looked up from the cutting board where she was grating cheddar cheese to sprinkle over bowls of chili.

"Everything's going wrong," Sam told her. "First Jen's accident, and now I've got a meeting at school tomorrow, and I have to spend all day Saturday working at Willow Springs—"

Hoping Gram would feel too sympathetic to scold her, Sam snatched a pinch of cheese and popped it in her mouth.

"Oh yes, dear," Gram said, as if she hadn't noticed. "I know what a chore you find it, working with wild horses all day."

"Yeah," Sam said, brushing aside her remark, "but at school, we're in charge of entertainment for a welcome back celebration the night before school starts."

"That sounds like fun! You could have a square dance," Gram suggested.

Sam froze. Was Gram joking?

It was a relief when she added, "Could you please start making a salad?"

Sam opened the refrigerator and stared inside.

She loved Gram as much as any person had ever loved a grandmother, but she couldn't imagine a lamer idea than a square dance.

Not that she'd say that, but since Gram was pretty good at reading her expressions, Sam leaned her head into the refrigerator a little farther than she had to, to grab the lettuce, green onions, and radishes she'd harvested from Gram's garden.

Sam arranged the salad ingredients on the kitchen counter. From the corner of her eye, it looked like Gram was waiting for a response to her idea.

"I don't think many kids my age know how to square dance."

For one horrible second, Sam got the feeling Gram would offer to teach her.

Sam kept talking. "And you know, it's kind of awkward at the beginning of the year. People don't know each other that well, and they might be too shy to dance with each other. . . . "

Gram tsked her tongue. "Whatever is there to be shy about? In square dancing you don't have to ask someone to dance. You're already assigned to a square. A square is four people—two boys and two girls—and then the caller tells you what to do."

What should she say now? Thank goodness a radish rolled off the counter. Sam dove to retrieve it from Cougar, who thought it might be a little red ball. Then she concentrated really hard on washing it.

"But, I suppose," Gram said, raising her voice, "if young people are used to just sitting around playing video games and watching television, dancing could be scary."

Sam bit her tongue and chopped the green onions with great precision. How had this happened? It just wasn't fair to be cornered into defending her entire generation.

Suddenly she saw an escape. She didn't like it, but it was better than nothing. And she knew Gram couldn't resist.

"I really want to take Ace out for a quick ride after dinner, but I know I've got all those school clothes and papers to go through. . . ."

"Yes indeed," Gram said, giving the chili a satisfied stir before she took bowls down from the cupboard.

"So, what if right after dinner I do that and then take him out?"

"That sounds fine to me," Gram said, "but you'll want to check with your father."

Sam planned to, but before they got dinner on the table, the phone rang again.

Sam looked at it accusingly. The last time it had rung, it had been Mr. Blair with his stupid assignment.

This morning, Jed had phoned to ask for help at Coffee Creek, and look how that had turned out. One superstitious portion of her brain suggested a return to the old days of ranch living, before there were telephone poles planted like trees across the range.

"Samantha, could you please answer that?" Gram asked.

"Only if you can promise me it's not somebody calling with something else horrible," Sam said.

Though Sam was half joking, Gram could have been a bit more sympathetic.

"They do say bad things come in threes," Gram offered.

"Great," Sam answered, but she wiped her wet hands on her jeans and picked up the receiver just the same.

Chapter Eleven ๑

"I'm still breathing."

"Jen!" Sam pressed the phone hard against her ear because her friend's voice was faint and muffled. "Don't even joke like that! Do you know how worried I've been?"

"Down, girl," Jen said. "My mom didn't even freak out like that."

"That's because she didn't see what I saw!" Sam took in a deep breath.

Why did she suddenly feel like crying? She hadn't cried when the bull was goring Jen. She hadn't cried when her most delicate touch had hurt Jen during a search for further injury, or when Jen's eyes locked on hers as she fastened the snug seat belt. Why now?

"And of course you're still breathing," Sam said. "That's not a bit funny."

"Will you stop?" Jen asked. Even injured and in the hospital, Jen sounded sensible.

"Yes," Sam told her.

"Good, because I didn't mean I was breathing as opposed to I'd *ceased* breathing because I was no longer alive. I meant that if the ragged end of my rib had punctured my lung, I might have sprung a leak. That can certainly hamper a girl's breathing."

"But are you all right?" Sam asked.

"As far as I know," Jen said. "They're being kind of secretive. That's why I called now. My mom and Mrs. Coley went down to the hospital coffee shop. I told them I wanted to take a nap and felt self-conscious while they were here."

"But you feel okay?"

"Really sore," Jen said, "like I've slept on the ground for a week — but I think they're, like, worried about my emotional state."

"You sound totally normal to me," Sam insisted. She listened to the rustling of sheets. Then, when she heard a little gasp of effort, she had to ask, "What are you doing?"

"Pulling the covers over my head so I can tell you the odd part," Jen whispered. "A doctor came by and asked me if I thought the bull was going to kill me —"

"Maybe he just has a morbid sense of cur —"

"—and how I *felt* about that."

"What did you say?"

"You would have been proud of me. I thought of a jillion smart-mouth answers and didn't use any of them. So, I don't know why the doctor got all huffy with me," Jen admitted.

"Tell me," Sam begged.

"Well, it was quite transparent what he was doing. . . . "

"Jen, just tell me."

"I said that I was sorry to disappoint him, but there was no need for a post-trauma interview because I hadn't been traumatized. I explained I'd been around cattle all my life and it wasn't like I was blinded by the attack. I could see you and Ross working to get the bull away from me, and I knew it was only a matter of holding out until you did."

"I can just imagine the look on the doctor's face," Sam said, and she could feel her smile fading as she thought of Ross.

But before she could urge Jen to repeat what she'd said to the doctor word for word to her dad, Jen gave a breathy laugh and kept whispering.

"I felt sort of bad," Jen admitted. "He was obviously expecting me to be this freaked-out child. So, I gave him something to write down."

Jen's voice sounded almost impish. Sam figured Jen must have given the poor doctor a dose of her usual sarcasm.

"What did you say?" Sam asked.

"I told him there *was* one dismal moment when it crossed my mind that I might not live long enough to see that bull made into hamburger."

Sam laughed as Jen added, "Then a nurse told him, 'These ranch girls are pretty tough cookies,' and that was when Mom came in and I got all teary and finally, it was like he'd seen what he was hoping for—"

"Jen, that's mean," Sam interrupted.

"Okay, at least what he was expecting, so he went away. He didn't even stay to hear about you slinging that pitchfork like it was a sledgehammer."

Sam's hands cramped as if she still gripped the wooden handle.

"It was all I could think of," she said.

"And it worked." Jen's faint words mixed with more rustling of sheets, as if she'd turned on her side to get more comfortable.

"Don't waste your thank-yous on me," Sam warned her.

"Even if you saved my life?" Jen asked sleepily.

"You would've done the same for me, any day, so just shut up," Sam said.

"Didn't anyone ever tell you that you're supposed to be nice to invalids?"

"Plenty of times," Sam began, but then Jen yawned.

She sounded so weak, Sam didn't have the heart to tell her friend about her father's anger toward Ross and his threat to home-school her again, or even about the welcome back night she'd probably miss.

"Let her rest," Gram whispered, and Sam glanced up to see that Brynna and Dad were already seated at the dinner table.

She'd been in another world while she talked with Jen, but this time Gram was right.

"Hey, Jen, save your strength," Sam said. "Later you can tell me what Ryan said when he got there."

"He brought me roses," Jen said, sighing, and then the phone clicked off.

It would have taken less time if Gram and Brynna hadn't both consulted with Sam on which clothes she had outgrown and which needed to be replaced, and if they hadn't wasted so many minutes criticizing her poor housekeeping.

"This room!" Gram had said, throwing her hands up in a gesture of despair.

"You should see her closet," Brynna had responded, as if Sam hadn't been standing right there. "She's been shoving stuff in there all summer."

She'd gotten off easy, though, Sam thought. If they only knew she'd been shoving stuff in her closet ever since she got home from San Francisco.

But once the clothes had been tried on and categorized, Sam still had time to go riding.

Perched on the edge of her bed, Sam tugged on her boots.

Gram had started back downstairs, and she was

bound to discover Sam hadn't talked with Dad yet about leaving for a ride on Ace.

Sam looked up to see that Brynna hadn't followed Gram.

"Get back by eight o'clock so you can crawl into bed early. I can take you to school for your Journalism meeting, but Rex asked me if I could make a nine o'clock counseling session," Brynna explained.

"Thanks," Sam told her.

That didn't give her much riding time, but Sam didn't complain. It would just soak up more time. She started for her bedroom door, rehearsing her conversation with Dad.

"Oh, and Wyatt said he'll help you on Saturday," Brynna said. "It'll be interesting to see how he and the Spanish Mustang get along before they know they're spending the rest of their lives together."

"Do you think we'll need Dad, too?"

"Well," Brynna said, "I thought since you wouldn't have Jen or Jake . . . "

Sam halted in her doorway. To keep from shouting at Brynna, Sam looked down at the horsehair bracelet on her wrist and wondered if Tempest was still wearing the braid she'd given her this morning.

It took her a full minute of turning the horsehair bracelet around on her wrist before she felt calm enough to ask, "I won't have Jake?"

"I told you," Brynna said uncertainly. "Didn't I?"

Sam shook her head. Brynna looked as dismayed

as she had earlier, when Dad had told her she'd for-gotten her doctor's appointment.

"I've just been so busy," Brynna said, and when she pressed the heels of her hands against her tem-ples, Sam knew she had no choice but to go easy on her stepmother.

"I know," Sam said.

"Maxine called my office this morning—no, I guess it was yesterday morning. Jake wanted to stay on at one of the colleges, in the dorm, for some special thing for prospective students. She's flying home to get ready for classes, but he's coming later because I said I could get along without him."

Of course Brynna could get along without Jake! She wasn't the one who'd been abandoned by both of her best friends. Sam knew they hadn't planned to ditch her—especially Jen—but knowing didn't make her feel less alone.

"I really thought I'd told you," Brynna said. "Sorry my brain's such a sieve."

"That's okay," Sam told her stepmother, but as she turned back toward the stairs, she was thinking about Gram's joke that bad things came in threes.

By the time she got downstairs, the view out the living room windows was amazing.

The long August twilight, casting purple shadows on the golden hills, was perfect for what Sam had in mind.

She could keep her promises to both Ace and

Tempest if she rode the gelding and ponied Tempest.

"Can I, Dad?" Sam asked after she'd explained her idea.

"She hasn't outgrown that halter yet?" Dad asked.

Although Dad hadn't answered her question, Sam answered his. Dad had made Tempest's soft leather halter with his own hands, after all, so maybe he was really curious, and not just stalling.

"She's on the second to last notch," Sam told him. Then she waited.

She knew he was hesitating because of Jen's accident. Caution over something he hadn't prevented was spilling over to something he could control. Sam crossed all the fingers she could.

Finally, Dad nodded.

"Don't take too long, though," he said. "Be back in the house in about an hour, okay?"

"Okay. Thanks, Dad," Sam said. She kissed Dad's cheek and hurried through the swinging door to the kitchen.

"Take Blaze with you," Gram told her.

"I will," Sam said, and kept heading toward the door as she heard Brynna's swift footsteps in the living room.

"And stay on this side of the river," her stepmother called.

"I will," Sam said, and she'd almost made it out the door when Dad shouted her name from the living room and she had to go back. Again.

Brynna stood beside him. Were they ganging up on her?

"Don't go near Fishbait Springs," Dad said. "Even if that's where your horse is hanging around, stay clear of it."

"I—what?" Sam asked. Maybe Brynna's scrambled thoughts were contagious. "You mean the bull, right?"

"No, I mean the horse. They're not likely to be there together," Dad said, "but Ross told me he's seen your gray there a time or two and Jed caught the bull there."

Weird, Sam thought. What could cause two such different animals to gravitate to the same place? And where was it?

Dad must have been musing over the same question.

"Probably wouldn't be a bad idea to ride out there in the next couple days and see what's attracting them to that spot," Dad said. "Can't be coincidence."

"I'm not sure I know where Fishbait Springs is," Sam said. Her pulse began hammering in her wrists as she thought of that bull and the Phantom together.

Dad folded his newspaper with a snap. His face hardened into his don't-be-getting-any-ideas look. He glanced toward the swinging door into the kitchen. Now Gram had come in, too.

"You were just by there this morning with Ross," Dad reminded Sam. "Don't you remember seeing your horse?"

Crossing her arms in irritation, because of course she remembered, Sam asked, "That little place on the *playa*? With the little clump of salt grass? I didn't see any spring."

"It's small," Dad said.

"I'll never forget that talk about raising shrimp out there," Gram said, laughing.

"Aquaculture," Brynna said. "I heard about that."

As the adults veered off onto this new tangent about something from years ago, Sam watched the grandfather clock's pendulum ticking off the minutes until dark.

"I better go," she said, and when no one stopped her, Sam bolted out the door, through the kitchen, and across the porch, then jogged toward the barn. She darted a quick glance toward the bunkhouse and saw that all three cowboys had come out onto their porch to escape the heat.

Please don't talk to me, please don't—

"Need some help?" Dallas called to her.

"No, thanks," Sam said, and kept going.

She caught and haltered Tempest, then saddled and bridled Ace faster than she thought possible.

When she approached the bunkhouse, ponying Tempest, the filly lifted her knees as if she were dancing to the tune Dallas played on the harmonica. Tempest was so excited to be going somewhere, she didn't seem to hear her mother calling after her.

Dallas motioned Sam to stop a minute. As she

slowed, she noticed Pepper was whittling and Ross seemed to be writing something in a leather-bound journal. Sam tried to catch his eyes, but Ross didn't look up. She couldn't imagine that he could see to write in the pale light that fell from the open bunkhouse door.

"Now will you take a look at that?" Pepper said, extending the chunk of wood he'd been carving toward Sam. "I've been working on it for three nights in a row and I bet you can't even tell what it is."

Sam couldn't.

"You've done a lot of work on it," Sam said.

More than anything, the scrap of wood resembled a legless pig, but she was pretty sure Pepper wouldn't carve such a thing.

"Not nice to put the boss's daughter on the spot like that," Dallas said, laughing.

"Okay, I'll tell you," Pepper said, giving in. "It's a swan—"

"Ohhh," Sam said.

"—with its head under its wing," Pepper added. "You know. Like they do when they're groomin' themselves."

"I can see that," Sam said.

"How could she not, when we get so many chances to watch swans around here," Dallas teased.

"I've been a few other places besides this ranch," Pepper protested.

Ross, sitting behind him, had been smiling as he

listened to the other two cowboys banter, but now, Sam noticed, the smile melted from his face. Was he thinking about the last place he'd been? Where he'd lost a job because of his stutter?

"Reason I called you over," Dallas said, as Sam raised her reins to ride on, "is it's the time of night that stallion used to come around. He liked the sound of this harmonica. Just be sure he doesn't spook that filly and get her to run off with him."

Sam shivered at the possibility.

"I'll be careful," Sam said.

But then her eyes caught a small movement. Ross gave a shrug so faint, no one noticed it but her. If this had been yesterday, she probably wouldn't have noticed, either, but a lot could change in a single day and that shrug was meant to tell her something.

I keep my eyes open, Ross had told her earlier today, and Sam was pretty sure he was hinting that the Phantom was no place near River Bend Ranch.

Chapter Twelve ❧

Blaze trotted alongside Ace, but he kept his eyes on Tempest.

Was her bay mustang glad the Border collie was babysitting the filly? Did he consider Tempest a burden Sam insisted on towing along behind them?

Sam couldn't tell, but Ace hadn't given a single testing buck or sidestep. He seemed to know Tempest was a baby, and so far he'd done nothing that might endanger her.

Dark Sunshine's anxious neighs only lasted a few minutes. As soon as they ended, Sam felt herself relax.

Hoofbeats, the rushing La Charla River, and a nighthawk swooping overhead acted like a magic spell.

Sam didn't know how, but her exhausting day evaporated once she rode Ace over the bridge into the warm August night.

When Sam realized there was no tension on the lead rope because Tempest was keeping up, she eased Ace into a jog, then a smooth lope. They rocked along the riverbank. Keeping her grip tight on the lead rope, Sam closed her eyes against the trailing fronds of a weeping willow tree.

Then she turned in her saddle. Glancing back over her shoulder, Sam saw Tempest held her head high and her brown eyes were wide. Nostrils flared, she sucked in scents of wild water and the plants that thrived beside it. The filly's black legs flashed ahead as she kept even with Ace's tail.

Tempest seemed to have forgotten her mother's neighs. She was glad to be galloping into new territory. Civilization hadn't robbed her of mustang longings, but Sam wasn't sure that was a good thing.

"Not that I can do anything about it," Sam muttered as she turned back to watch the twilight world through the frame of Ace's ears.

Sam let herself think about Saturday. She felt a surge of excitement as she pictured adoption day at Willow Springs. She'd see people peer into the holding corrals and fall in love with wild horses. She'd see them wait to hear if their numbers were called and listen while families agonized over what they could bid on the horses they wanted most. It wasn't a perfect solution, Sam thought, but if the mustangs couldn't run free, living with human partners was the next best thing.

At a snort behind her, Sam slowed Ace a little.

She looked back to see that Tempest had spotted a lone Canada goose. Black wings outstretched, it cruised above the surface of the river. The filly's legs kept pace with Ace, but her head had swung to track the bird.

The goose was so near, when it banked away from the river, Sam heard air currents whispering through its feathers.

Ace snorted at the bird, then arched his neck and maintained a smooth gait so that Tempest didn't crash into him while she was distracted.

Legs firm against the saddle, Sam leaned forward and rubbed the back of her rope hand against Ace's neck. Years in the wild had taught Ace not every unexpected thing needed to be feared.

She wished everyone considering one of the horses from BLM's adoption program could see him in action.

As her thoughts turned to Saturday's adoption day, Sam felt glad that she'd get to see Inez Garcia, the trainer of movie horses, again. Inez had promised that Sam could help her pick out a stablemate for Bayfire. That would be fun.

Even better than that, Dad would meet his new horse. Sam crossed her fingers that all would go well.

At the slower pace, Tempest zigzagged behind Ace. She darted left, then right, her movements quick and random as a fish on a line.

A rumble from Ace did nothing to calm her, so Sam tried talking to the young animal.

"Calm down, crazy girl," Sam told the filly. "You'll use up all your energy before we get home."

But it wasn't Sam's scolding that ended the filly's dance.

Blaze stopped. Body tense and ears raised, his ruff a flash of white in the deepening dusk, Blaze stared across the La Charla River.

Sam tightened her left hand on the reins and Ace halted, mirroring Blaze's tense pose.

Tempest didn't seem to care what they'd heard. The filly dropped her head level with her knees. Breathing hard, she took advantage of the time to rest.

Sam stared through the violet-gray night, but nothing moved on the far riverbank.

"What is it, guys?"

She listened hard. Just beyond the rushing of the river, there was something. Maybe the yips of hunting coyotes.

Blaze trembled with eagerness, as if he'd launch his body into the river and swim across. He looked up at Sam and whined, asking for permission to abandon her.

Sam remembered last spring, when the dog kept

sneaking off, disappearing for days and worrying them. She'd heard of ranch dogs being lured off and eaten by coyotes, but could they play together, too?

Blaze had always come back. . . .

Sam thought of what Brynna had said this morning, about giving children roots and wings. Did that apply to animals, too? Should she tell Blaze to go on and play, or should she keep him safe with her? She couldn't forget Brynna had instructed her to take Blaze along to give Tempest some protection, too.

"Stay," Sam ordered.

Panting, Blaze sat and waited.

Darkness was falling fast, and though Sam wasn't afraid of coyotes, she felt a little nervous. A pack of coyotes had probably never attacked a horse, rider, and domestic dog all together, but Tempest might attract their attention.

Even though she was tired, the filly was unpredictable. If she managed to jerk loose from Sam's grip and run, the coyotes would give chase. Through their yellow predator eyes, Tempest would look like a small prey animal. She could be surrounded and hurt before Sam could get to her.

Determined that would never happen, Sam wrapped the lead rope a few more turns around her saddle horn and clutched it tightly.

"We're going home," Sam told the animals. "This baby's worn out and I'll be in trouble if I don't hurry back."

Before he answered the pressure of her legs against the saddle, Ace's neck curved and he stretched to touch noses with Tempest.

The black filly trembled, but she didn't back away from the bigger horse.

"You're going to be just like your dad, aren't you?" Sam said as Tempest matched Ace's greeting. "I don't know whether that makes me happy or not."

River Bend's porch light shone through the darkness. Ace moved slowly and surely toward it, while Tempest meandered at the end of her lead rope.

By the time they reached the bridge over the La Charla River, Tempest's hooves scuffed with drowsiness.

They rode into the quiet ranch yard and through the beam of porch light. Blaze bolted for the bunkhouse, and Sam glanced after him to see Ross sitting there, alone.

Sam noticed Dad leaning with arms folded against the front door of the ranch house. She was a little late, but Dad just nodded, satisfied that she was safely home.

Sam slung Ace's reins over the hitching rail to hold him while she hurried Tempest back to her mother. She returned to strip off his saddle. By porch light, she gave him a quick grooming, then turned him out into the ten-acre pasture.

Not until Sam walked into the tack room, yawning

and wishing that her saddle weren't so heavy, did she see the paper tucked through her empty saddle rack.

A misplaced bridle or halter, even a jacket someone had taken off and hung there and then forgotten would have made sense, but a piece of paper didn't.

Eager to hang up her saddle and get back to the house, Sam almost ignored it, but the back of her hand brushed the paper as she lifted her saddle onto its rack.

Folded lengthwise, the sheet of paper poked Sam's hand with such insistence, she had to retrieve it.

It wasn't lined notebook paper or a gridded sheet from Gram's ledger. The paper was a little stiff, a bit textured, and in the barn's dim light, kind of ivory-colored. When she pulled the two halves back, a crease remained down the center, and she could see three groups of words.

This didn't have the random look of her mother's to-do list that she'd found a few months ago. Carefully spaced apart, they looked like . . . three poems?

Quickly, Sam glanced around the barn. She was alone, as she'd known she would be, but this was weird. The paper had been left on her saddle rack. Whoever had written these words must have meant for her to read them.

The handwritten letters were tough to read in the half-light.

Forget it. She wouldn't try to puzzle them out

here. She'd take them back to the house. Sam folded the sheet lengthwise again and tucked it inside the waistband of her jeans.

Dad was gone from the porch when she reached it. In fact, when Sam passed through the living room, he barely looked up from the television comedy he was watching with Brynna and Gram.

Sam sprinted up the stairs to read the poems someone had left behind.

A mew from Cougar, who'd centered his soft body on the patchwork star on her bedspread, greeted her.

"Hi," Sam said, then closed the door soundly and scanned the painstaking printing.

Her first impression had been right. They were three poems.

She thought of Ross sitting on the bunkhouse porch, writing. They must be his, but why wouldn't he say something—no, of course he wouldn't say something. For the tough, quiet cowboy who stammered under stress, talking about his poetry would be harder than facing a charging bull. But why would he share his poetry with her?

Cowboy poetry gatherings were held all over the West. Real buckaroos and dudes wrote about horses and hardship, and the West's beauty. Lots more wrote humorous rhymes about cantankerous critters and days that just went all wrong. So Ross didn't have to be embarrassed by his creativity.

Still, she couldn't see him sharing his work with Pepper or Dallas. Look at the way Dallas had joshed with Pepper over his carving. And even though Pepper might possibly understand, Sam couldn't imagine Ross pulling together the words to explain what he was doing and ask Pepper for his critique.

So he'd left these for her.

One of the poems was titled "Alkali Pegasus." It just had to be about the Phantom.

She folded the sheet before she could be sure. She wanted to savor the words and make them last.

Sam forced herself to shower. After she'd dried off and pulled on a summer nightgown, she thought how weird it was that Ross was a writer. Of course she knew poets could come from anywhere, but she was still surprised.

And—*Pegasus*. She'd thought of her horse that way, but she'd never guessed anyone else had.

Sam brushed her teeth and laid out her clothes for the next day, before sitting cross-legged on her bed with Ross's poetry.

Disturbed by her flouncing around, Cougar stalked to the end of her bed. With regal care, he sat, then raised a striped paw up to his mouth. He licked it busily, as if he didn't really care if he was her audience.

"I can't help it. I've got to read 'Alkali Pegasus,' first," she told the cat.

Sam took a deep breath, exhaled, then drew another breath and read in a whisper.

"Silver stallion soar
Past summer sage, sandstorms, clouds.
Fly me with you. High."

She let the words drift into the far corners of the
room as she read it silently to herself a second time.
Then, Sam rushed on to the next one.

"It's called 'Valentine to River Bend Ranch,'" Sam
said out loud. "Have you ever heard of writing a
Valentine to a place? No? Well, here you go, Cougar.

"'Don't sink your heart here.
It's another man's land, boy.'
Too late. Heart's Done Gone."

Sam lowered the sheet of poems and sighed. Then
she hugged herself against the shivers the poem
stirred.

Ross loved this ranch. She felt her own sad smile
as she imagined Ross shaking his head and writing
Heart's Done Gone.

"Mrow," Cougar complained. Then he batted at
the paper and made it scuttle over the quilt.

"Be patient," Sam told him. "There's just one
more."

Cougar curled up, facing away from her. Sam
cleared her throat, but the cat thumped his tail in
irritation.

"It's called 'Echo,' and it's just like the others. It only has three lines, and—hey!"

Sam slapped one hand down with a padded thump on her quilt.

These poems were haiku! She'd learned to write the verses when she was in middle school.

Sam shook her head and touched the paper, counting five syllables in the first line of each poem, seven in the middle lines, then five in the last ones.

How many "who would've guessed" moments could one person have in a day? Not only was Ross a sagebrush poet, he wrote in a form from Japan!

"Can you believe this?" Sam whispered, in disbelief. She read "Echo" to herself.

Neigh—mares come runnin'
Nicker—spring foals feel safe, warm
Speak—for the silent.

Sam swallowed. At first, she'd thought the poem was about the Phantom's family. It probably was, but there seemed to be something else there, too. She thought of the way Ross had struggled not to stammer as he tried to tell Jed about Jen's accident. The Phantom's nickers and neighs seemed effortless by comparison.

And the first poem, Sam thought, eyes zipping back to the top of the page, asked the stallion to fly him away.

Sam placed the poetry on her bedside table and crawled under her covers. It was just a little too chilly to sleep without them tonight.

She yawned. She tried to think of Ross and the Phantom and make sense of what the big cowboy felt for the wild horse, but she was asleep before she could.

Chapter Thirteen ❧

"Fall is in the air," Brynna chirped. She looped her arm through Sam's as they walked toward the BLM truck.

Brynna had agreed to drop Sam off at school. Dad and Gram assumed Brynna was on her way to work, and she hadn't corrected them. There was no reason they needed to know she was driving into Reno to be counseled by her boss. At least, not until the Spanish Mustang was theirs.

Sam's stomach growled. She'd turned down breakfast partly because she'd grabbed a few more minutes of sleep, and partly because the corned beef hash and eggs Gram had made for breakfast looked gross.

Of course, they were probably delicious, but she felt cranky because she had to go back to school early, without her best friends.

Hooves thundered and a sharp whinny came from the saddle horses as they galloped in their morning stampede around the ten-acre pasture. Blaze raced along the fence barking, and the high desert air smelled like apple cider.

Sam lived in the best place in the world, and she was allowing Brynna to drive her away from it. On purpose.

"I hate fall," Sam said.

She didn't really, but the sight of the horses cavorting in the crisp morning reminded her that most mornings, for the next ten months, she wouldn't have time to enjoy the horses.

She'd be too busy figuring out who'd give her a ride to the bus stop, or moping over math homework she hadn't understood.

But Brynna ignored Sam's pouting.

"I love it," Brynna said. "Cool nights and bright days, the horses are frisky, we can watch football, go to back-to-school sales—"

"That's just it. Back. To. School," Sam moaned.

"You won't believe me, but I miss going back to school," Brynna said. "Each year I envy students and teachers."

"Maybe you don't remember what it's like," Sam hinted.

"I do remember," Brynna said. "Once a year, you get a totally fresh start. In most jobs, you just plod along with the same people. All of them know what you've done right, and wrong, and you're kind of . . ." Brynna searched her mind for the right word. "*Shackled* by it.

"But each class you walk into this year, you'll probably have a new teacher, someone who knows nothing about you—and even if the other kids have heard your name, most of *them* won't know you, either. It's a chance to set goals and be a new you."

She let Brynna keep talking, but Sam was pretty sure she wouldn't be convinced to love going back to school.

Then a worrisome thought popped into her mind.

"What's wrong with the old me?" Sam asked.

"Nothing," Brynna said. "If you don't count the paranoia."

Sam stuck out her tongue at Brynna. Her stepmother mirrored the bratty expression, and they both laughed.

"No, there's nothing wrong with the old you," Brynna repeated, "but isn't there something you didn't accomplish last year that you regret? Just a teeny bit?"

"I can't think of anything," Sam said. Before climbing into the truck, she turned to Blaze, cupped his face in her hands, and kissed his muzzle. She'd miss hanging out with him, too.

The trip to Darton High didn't take nearly as long

as Sam had hoped. When they arrived, the school looked deserted.

"Sorry you're so early," Brynna said as she pulled up in front and peered over the school's freshly black-topped parking lot. Only three vehicles were parked there. "And I might be a little late picking you up. I'll call when I'm on my way back."

"I hope the phone number in the journalism room is the same," Sam said.

"It will be," Brynna said. Then she leaned over as far as her seat-belted pregnancy would allow and gave Sam a quick kiss on the cheek. "Have fun, honey."

Sam stood in front of Darton High School.

An early morning breeze rustled the American flag and pinged the flag's pulley against the metal flagpole.

Sam took a deep breath. She could almost taste the fresh-cut lawns edged back neatly from the concrete walks that crisscrossed the school.

She took the gray path leading toward A Building. That's where she'd find Mr. Blair's classroom—the J room, as he called it. That had caused her a few panicky moments as a freshman, until she realized it didn't fit with the school's A, B, and C building plan. It just stood for Journalism.

And this year, she knew that.

As she walked, Sam noticed that the sprinklers had wet the concrete more than the lawns.

Just like last year, Sam thought, and the idea made her smile.

She was a sophomore. Freshman year had ended. Even without Jen and Jake, she knew her way around the campus.

Just like it had last night, Sam's mind flashed back to Brynna telling Dad something about giving kids roots and wings.

Maybe Brynna had a point, and maybe, Sam thought, she had put down roots at Darton High last year, and this year she could "fly" a little.

What if she tried out for a sport? Or even for a part in a play? What if she talked to more kids in her classes, so she'd have at least one person to call if she didn't have the homework assignment? And what if she learned why Mr. Weaver, the chemistry teacher, was always tending that bush of bloodred roses outside B Building?

There he was now, kneeling and clipping away at something around the rosebush's base.

"Hello, Mr. Weaver," Sam called, her voice echoing in the silence.

The teacher wore a vacant smile as he waved. He probably couldn't guess he was her best friend's favorite teacher.

But that was okay, Sam thought.

She hugged last year's journalism notebook a little closer against her chest. That made her look down at what she'd decided to wear, and Sam wondered if she'd made a good choice.

She was wearing her second-best jeans with a khaki-colored tank top and a necklace strung with shells. Aunt Sue had bought the necklace for her at Fisherman's Wharf in San Francisco, insisting the flame-colored hearts of the shells matched Sam's auburn hair.

Now that her hair had grown out so that the ends brushed her collarbone, maybe someone would notice.

Or not, Sam reprimanded herself.

Being self-conscious was something she wanted to leave behind in her freshman year. Starting now, she'd just be herself, not agonize over why that wasn't okay.

With one hand, Sam pushed open the door to A Building and murmured to herself, "Ready or not, here I come."

It wasn't possible that the scrubbed corridor walls and banks of closed lockers were holding their breath in anticipation. But that's what it felt like as Sam hurried down the mirror-buffed floors toward the journalism room.

She couldn't wait to be inside a familiar classroom. When she reached Mr. Blair's room, she saw he still had black paper taped over the window in his door, to keep passing students from peering in at their friends and disrupting their concentration.

Sam couldn't tell before she twisted the doorknob whether anyone was inside.

They were.

Mr. Blair sat at his big wooden desk, gripping a pen while he considered the stacks of papers that already surrounded him.

Rjay, the *Darton Dialogue*'s student editor, was sprawled over two desks in front of him.

They both looked up as Sam walked in, then tugged the door closed behind her.

"It's kind of creepy out there," Sam said. Then, without thinking, she dragged a desk close to Rjay's and basked in the smiles of welcome.

"Greetings. Today is the beginning of the end. At least for me," Rjay said.

Before Sam could puzzle out what he meant, Rjay described the summer he'd spent living in a trailer on his aunt's sheep ranch, cutting brush—he displayed scratched arms for proof—disentangling "wild woolies" from thorn thickets, studying for college entrance exams, and earning money for contact lenses.

"So what do you think, Forster?" Rjay asked. He leaned toward her, blinking, and Sam realized why the gawky senior looked different. His wire-rimmed glasses were gone. "Are they worth it?"

Maybe Brynna was right, Sam thought while she tried to think of what to say. Maybe people liked recreating themselves over the summer.

"She's speechless," Rjay said to Mr. Blair, but

he looked a little anxious.

"Because you're a new man," Sam said, and when that seemed to cheer him, she added, "I hardly recognized you."

"Now he'll be insufferable," Mr. Blair complained as Rjay punched a fist into the air.

Sam laughed, but Rjay's first statement, about it being the beginning of the end, had just sunk in.

"You're a senior, too," Sam said. Just like Jake, Rjay would be leaving.

"Yep, I'll be gone," Rjay said, with mock melancholy. Then he held up his index finger as if a bright thought had flashed into his brain. "But Rachel Slocum's only a junior. After I'm gone, you'll have her for company."

"She's in Journalism again?" Sam yelped. She shot a quick look at Mr. Blair, but the teacher was pretending to be busy.

"Alas, yes," Rjay said, "despite her threats not to return if she wasn't appreciated, she's back."

This time Mr. Blair did speak up. "Save the sniping for the first bell, can you, kids?"

Sam decided that was good advice. It was possible Rachel had changed during summer, too.

As it turned out, Rachel didn't show up for the back-to-school meeting.

Mr. Blair had asked all the Journalism students to pull desks into a circle before he'd called roll. When Rachel Slocum didn't answer, her friend

Daisy, a cheerleader who was back in Journalism to make up an F she'd earned during the first semester of last school year, did.

"She's not finished with her voice lessons," Daisy said, as if everyone in the room—or perhaps the state—should have known.

"I thought she was in Europe," said Cammy. Ringleted and blonde, she was another of Rachel's followers.

"Duh," Daisy said. "That was in July, and this is August."

Dizzied by the prospect of having Rachel and two of her fans in the class, Sam raised her eyebrows toward Rjay, then smiled at Zeke, who'd been on the *Darton Dialogue* staff last year. They gave her sympathetic eye rolls, and another girl smiled, too.

Sam recognized her, but what was her name?

She had flyaway brownish-blond hair and violet veins that showed in her hands and temples. She was taller than Sam, but for some reason, Sam always thought that if Ally—that was it, Ally McClintock!— were reduced to the size of a pencil, she'd look like a fairy.

She didn't know Ally very well, but recognized her from church. Sam was pretty sure Ally's dad was the choir director.

So there. She knew another person!

When Mr. Blair finished explaining their assignment for back-to-school night, there was silence except for a lawn mower running outside the classroom window.

"Okay," Rjay said. "Everyone write down as many entertainment ideas as you can think of on a scrap of paper. Then wad up the paper and throw it at me. Not too enthusiastically," he cautioned. "And I'll read them out."

It was a great idea, Sam thought, but staring at her paper didn't make any ideas materialize.

Without looking, Sam could tell only two people were jotting down ideas. Ally was sitting across from her. Sam watched her pale fingers fly as she wrote all kinds of things. Cammy was doing the same.

"Listen, people, you have to have at least one idea. Write it down. No one will know it's yours."

For some reason Sam could think of nothing except poor Jen, lying in the hospital with her rib broken by a bull, so when Rjay called "Time!", the only thing Sam could scribble down was rodeo.

She guessed it was better than square dancing, but when Rjay uncrumpled her paper and read "rodeo" aloud, everyone looked at her.

Sam folded her hands on her desk and looked back. She could take a few knowing stares. Anything was better than Rachel's sneers about smelly horses and smellier cowgirls.

"All right," Rjay said, "this calls for a vote. Just a show of hands," he emphasized when Cammy began tearing another sheet of paper from her notebook.

"We have suggestions for a pie-eating contest, a kiss-the-pig contest—what's that, exactly? Anyone?"

"Each teacher in the school has a jar with his or her name on it," Ally explained, "and then all the students put pennies or whatever in the jar of the teacher they want to see kiss a pig, and then, whichever teacher's jar has the most money . . . "

"I get it," Rjay said, nodding, and then he read, "talent show, talent show again, videos in the gym, mud wrestling in the girls' locker room—" He broke off when most of the girls groaned and stared at Zeke.

"What?" Zeke demanded. "I suggested videos."

"No you didn't. I did," Daisy snapped.

"Rodeo," Rjay continued, "and teachers versus students basketball game. All really entertaining, but now it's time to vote."

Rjay read off each suggestion again, and when the voting ended, there were thirteen votes for the talent show and one for mud wrestling.

A bustle of organization followed, with everyone promising to call ten people, hoping they'd get at least that many to perform.

"How many of you can volunteer right now?" Mr. Blair asked.

The same silence descended, until Rjay said, "I could shear sheep."

The laughter that followed was interrupted by Ally, who said she could play the guitar; a new boy, who said he knew Philippine stick fighting, which looked really cool on stage; two girls who knew a funny skit; and Zeke, who said he might be able to work out a skateboard routine.

"I used to twirl," Cammy said. "Batons," she clarified when Rjay looked confused. "If we were really desperate, I could do that."

"Forster?" Mr. Blair asked.

Sam shrugged. "I could tack up a couple of my photographs, but that's not very entertaining. Really, that's my only talent." When Mr. Blair continued staring at her, she added, "If you give me some markers, I can make signs pointing the way to the talent show."

Once Mr. Blair was satisfied, he handed everyone copies of their class schedules.

"This is your perk for showing up early," he said, but by then no one was listening.

Sam's schedule was no surprise. In fact, it was a lot like last year's schedule, except that she had geometry instead of algebra, world history instead of American history, and Life Skills in place of P.E.

The meeting was breaking up, and people were offering one another rides home, while Sam stared at the class telephone and wished Brynna would call to say she was on her way, when Ally paused next to Sam's desk.

The first thing Sam noticed was that Ally was chewing on an already short thumbnail.

"Hi," Sam said, smiling.

"Hi. I, uh, have a favor to ask, and I know I hardly know you at all, but you, well, look friendlier than—" Ally groaned. "Look, I'm in charge of the preschool choir at church, you know?"

"The Cherubs," Sam said. "They're really cute."

"Thanks, but see, my mom usually helps me with them. She lines them up and makes sure everyone's shoes are tied and stuff like that, but Mom is at a conference in Iowa, and since you come to church most Sundays, anyway . . ."

"Sure," Sam said, "no problem. I'd be glad to help."

"She's a cowgirl, after all, and she already knows how to herd them little doggies." Daisy giggled. Then she hurried toward the classroom door.

Great. Rachel's followers had gotten gutsier over the summer, Sam lamented silently.

But Zeke didn't let the cheerleader get away with flinging out an insult, then taking off.

"You're really funny, Daisy," Zeke said, following right on Daisy's heels.

"Go away," Daisy said, glancing back with a cold stare.

"No, I mean it," Zeke insisted, and even as they went out the door, Sam could still hear him. "Maybe you could tell jokes at the talent show or, hey, you're such a comedian, maybe you could get your own show. Yeah, that's it. . . ."

"Leave me alone." Daisy's voice echoed from down the hall.

"Thanks!" Ally said to Sam, then, "See you Sunday."

Sam leaned back in her desk chair. She felt useful, and pleased that she'd become friendly with Ally. Today was turning into a much better day than yesterday had been. So much better that she just knew tomorrow, Dad's birthday, would be perfect. He'd fall in love with the spirited little Spanish Mustang, and they'd all live happily ever after.

Chapter Fourteen ❧

Before her eyes opened, Sam heard Brynna singing "Happy Birthday" and thought that was a promising way to start the day.

"Your birthday surprise comes a little later." Brynna's voice carried down the hall.

"You feelin' up for all this work today?" Dad asked.

"Most of it's done. I'm just supervising," Brynna confessed. "Sorry I've got to leave for Willow Springs so early."

Cheek against her pillow, Sam smiled. Dad's birthday present from Brynna would be a big surprise, all right. She just hoped he liked it.

As far as Sam knew, Dad hadn't questioned

Brynna's need for him today. He figured he was filling in for Jake and Jen, and he aimed to do it with style.

Last night, he'd suggested he and Sam would both ride gentled mustangs to show off wild horses' potential.

The idea had been such a turnaround from Dad's criticism of wild horses just two days before, both Brynna and Sam had jumped up from the dinner table and hugged him, meeting each other's eyes over Dad's head.

"Don't think it means nothin', 'cause it don't," Dad had grumbled, but when he'd gone to hitch the horse trailer to his truck, Sam had felt a celebration of excitement fizz through her. Dad and the Spanish Mustang just might become partners.

Sam's eyes locked on her alarm clock. It was nearly six A.M. and she and Dad were supposed to leave by six-thirty.

She eased out of bed, grabbed the present she'd decided was too pretty to wrap, and padded down the hall to Dad and Brynna's bedroom.

Dad turned at the sound of her bare feet on the creaky wooden floor boards.

Shaved, dressed in pressed jeans and a fresh white shirt with tiny blue stripes, he stood in front of the mirror in his dim bedroom, slicking his dark hair back with water.

Sam paused in the doorway.

The first things she noticed were Dad's leather

chinks and vest arranged neatly on the bed. He'd rubbed leather softener into them last night, and they smelled like a brand-new saddle.

The first thing *Dad* noticed was his present.

"Happy birthday, Daddy," Sam said.

"Well, what's this now?" Dad asked.

His grin widened, white against his tanned face, as he took the blue silk square. He held it with both hands, examining the brands and her handwork as if it were a museum treasure. Finally, he looked up.

"You don't mean to tell me you did all this fine stitching?"

Sam nodded.

"Honey, have you ever done anything like this before?" Dad was in awe.

"Gram helped me," she said, and then, because she was a little embarrassed, Sam added, "And it'll match what you're wearing."

"That it will," Dad said. He draped the scarf around his neck. "If you stand there and watch me tie this in the mirror, I think you'll be able to do this for yourself."

Dad's fingers moved slowly as he explained the complicated horsetail knot buckaroos used to tie the scarves they called "wild rags," but Sam wasn't really listening. She wasn't even looking in the mirror.

Sam was admiring the pair of blue wings she'd stitched on this side of the scarf and wondering when Dad would understand why she'd sewn them there.

Dad shoveled down the birthday waffles Gram had made him, faster than Sam could. When she got outside, he'd already loaded Popcorn and Ace into the trailer.

"We're ready to go," he said. "I'm just going to grab a cup of coffee to drink while I drive. Want me to get you some more cocoa?"

"No thanks," Sam said. Even though Dad would be there to help her, she suddenly felt a burden of responsibility.

What if she let a horse escape and it stampeded through the crowds and everyone changed their minds about adopting such dangerous animals? What if someone asked her to read a freeze brand and she couldn't? Sure, she knew how to look up the code, but would they expect her to have it memorized?

Before she could make herself more nervous, she spotted Ross dawdling near the ten-acre pasture.

Dawdling? Ross?

Of course, he wanted to know what she'd thought about his poetry.

Sam rushed across the ranch yard. She could see his blush even before she reached him, and his knuckles turned white from gripping the top fence rail.

"They were wonderful!" Sam said. "Perfect. Anyone reading them would know what it's like to be here."

Face turning a deep burgundy red, Ross looked away from her.

"D-don't know what you're t-t-talkin' about."

Sam didn't let his denial stop her.

"You've got to take them to a cowboy poetry festival and—" Sam broke off, wishing she could suck the words back inside her lips. If she'd punched Ross in the stomach, he couldn't have looked more surprised.

"N-never h-h-happen," Ross said.

His suddenly opened, then clamped-shut mouth and quick shake of his head was disappointment, Sam realized. He'd trusted her to know that would be impossible for him. If she was nervous getting up in front of people, Ross was terrified.

Okay, Sam thought. He'd kind of admitted they were his poems, but he didn't want to talk about them. She could understand that. And she couldn't let him regret he'd showed his poems to her.

Sam's mind raced, trying to think of a way to mend Ross's discomfort.

"Hey, my dad said that was Fishbait Springs where we saw the Phantom yesterday." Sam rushed her words into the silence.

Ross gave a faint nod. "I been askin' him what he lost out there."

It was a funny thing to say, but the kitchen door banged shut and Sam blurted out her real worry before Dad made her leave.

"That's where that Hazard bull hangs out."

"It is?" Ross drew a deep breath.

"Jed told Dad he's a loner, and that's his territory

and I know stallions and bulls don't pick fights with each other, but he's—"

"Got a kinked thinker," Ross said, tapping his head.

As Dad strode up, Ross touched the brim of his hat and moved away.

"Let's go," Dad said, and then, in the slamming of doors and crunch of tires on dirt, he added, "Hope Jed lets him off the hook."

"He has to," Sam said, but it was clear from Dad's silent nod that he didn't want to talk about it anymore.

He sipped his coffee and drove, while Sam's mind darted from thoughts of the Spanish Mustang, to Inez Garcia, to wondering if Ace's first days off the range had been at Willow Springs.

Only when they were through Thread the Needle, with the wild horse center in sight, did Dad say, "About Ross's poems—"

"You know about them?" Sam asked.

"Saw some papers stickin' in your saddle rack after you left last night and had a look at 'em. Since Ross is always writin' in that book of his . . ." Dad shrugged.

Sam wondered how much she could say to Dad without betraying Ross's trust in her.

"They're really good," she said.

The truck moved along for another two minutes before Dad said, "It'd be a real gift for someone to read 'em for him, say at the Cowboy Poetry Gathering in Elko."

"Don't look at me!" Sam gasped. She waved her hands as if she could banish Dad's words from the air between them. "I'm no performer, and I'm no cowboy. Why don't you do it? Or Pepper or Dallas or—"

"Don't look for it to get done, then," Dad said with a snort of laughter. Then, as the gates to Willow Springs Wild Horse Center swung open, he gave her a wink. "It was just worth a try."

Inez Garcia's nose was peeling and her black hair streamed loose over her shoulders. She wore slim-fitting jeans, a tailored shirt, and silver hoop earrings just like she had the day she and her stunt horse Bayfire had arrived at River Bend Ranch. Unlike that day, she now looked relaxed and excited.

"Too bad Bayfire couldn't be here," Sam said.

"He'd be a handful," Inez said. "He's been enjoying his down time and has started acting like a bossy stallion again. But he's trusting me to pick out his stablemate."

As soon as the front gates had swung open to the public at eight-thirty, Sam had spotted Inez. The Hollywood trainer had given Ace a hug, then stood anxiously with a crowd of other potential adopters on the small lawn in front of the Willow Springs office building while Brynna's boss, Rex Black, drew names and assigned numbers, then explained the silent bidding process.

Tall and trim, wearing a tailored shirt tucked into khaki pants, Rex Black looked more like an athlete than an office worker. Somewhere in her memory, Sam had filed the information that he was a marathon runner and a stickler for rules and regulations. Brynna had probably mentioned that at the dinner table one night. Considering he'd required Brynna to be counseled before she adopted a wild horse, Sam was pretty sure she was right about that "stickler for details" part.

Sam twisted in her saddle, looking for Dad. If he spotted Brynna out of uniform, he might guess something was up. Her eyes scanned the crowd. A man on a white horse shouldn't be very hard to find.

He wasn't.

Dad sat astride Popcorn, letting a group of children pet the albino gelding. But it was *where* he'd stopped that made Sam glad. It had to be more than good luck that Popcorn stood beside the corral holding the Spanish Mustang, and Dad was watching the horses inside as if he couldn't look away.

Yes! Sam thought. By the end of the day, there'd be a new horse on River Bend Ranch.

Since the adoption day seemed to be running smoothly, Sam reined Ace alongside Brynna and Inez and listened as Brynna led the trainer on a walking tour around Willow Springs and explained how the horses up for adoption were chosen.

"We've picked horses with good conformation and put them up front," Brynna explained. "And with this"—Brynna touched the paperwork Inez had already picked up—"you can match the number on the horse's tag"—Brynna pointed to the braided red-and-white ropes that held a numbered tag around each horse's neck—"to the list and find out its age, which herd management area it came from, and things like that. These horses are from Rock Creek, and those are from the Little Humboldt area."

"I hope it's all right to say I'm impressed," Inez said. "These are good-looking horses." She looked up quickly at Sam. "Not that Ace isn't. You know I think he's wonderful."

"And it has nothing to do with the fact that he looks a lot like Bayfire," Sam joked.

"Of course not," Inez said. "And I know the ones we saw running free were beautiful, but I was afraid, living here like they do, they might be kind of scrubby and dirty."

Brynna didn't take offense. Even though she was out of uniform, she acted like the professional she was, and Sam knew she'd heard remarks like Inez's before.

"The horses will roll and give themselves dust baths. If the corrals aren't muddy to begin with, that keeps them pretty clean."

They walked on.

"My friend Jen sure wanted to meet you," she

told Inez. As Sam thought of Jen, she felt a heaviness in her chest.

Inez shrugged as if it were no big deal. "Let's do it." She looked around as if she could spot Jen.

"She's not here. She had an accident and she's in the hospital," Sam said.

"I'm so sorry," Inez said. "I hope it's nothing serious."

Sam drew a breath to explain, but she was glad when Brynna took over and told Inez what had happened.

When Brynna had finished, Inez shook her head.

"It's not like in the movies," Inez said. "We'd wear all kinds of protective gear for a stunt like that. Give me her address, though, Sam." Inez paused and dug through her leather purse for a small notebook. Then she looked up with a grin. "I'll have Bayfire send her something fun."

It was a good thing Sam talked quickly, she thought, because a minute later, Inez stopped as if she'd been turned to plaster. Motionless, she stared into a corral.

"She's pretty," Inez said. "The red sorrel that looks like Raggedy Ann—isn't she great?"

"Now she's one we *did* have to pull a few foxtails and cockleburs out of," Brynna said, and Sam spotted the horse.

The bright sorrel's corkscrew-curled mane and wavy coat made her stand out from the other mares.

When Inez kept staring as if hypnotized by the horse, Brynna added, "In some areas we have a few horses with curly Bashkir blood."

Clearly, Inez had found her horse. She stood at the fence, watching the mare with fascination. Sam tried to meet Brynna's eyes, but her stepmother was distracted by some activity across the corrals and open areas, over near her office.

"Can you tell what's going on?" Brynna asked Sam. "I hear raised voices, but I can't see."

Even looking in that direction from the saddle, Sam couldn't figure it out. She stood in her stirrups.

"Maybe someone just put a really high bid on a horse?" Sam suggested. Then she drew in a breath. "I hope it's not the Spanish Mustang."

"I don't think that's it," Brynna said, "but I plan to find out."

"Let me just ride over there and see," Sam said, but Brynna probably didn't even hear her. "Inez, we'll talk to you later," Sam said.

"Okay," Inez agreed without looking away from the horse. "I've found my girl."

Even though she wasn't officially working, Brynna strode toward the commotion as if she was in charge.

Sam tried to follow right behind Brynna, but she drew rein to call back at the stunt trainer.

"Inez, you better hurry and put your bid on the sheet," Sam said.

Slowly, Inez tightened her ponytail, then looked at Sam as if she needed to translate what she'd said.

Then, Inez's eyes started open and she bolted toward Brynna's office and the posted bid sheets. She moved so fast that, even though Sam was mounted, Inez beat her there.

By the time Sam reached the office building, Inez had already marked down her bid on the curly red mare, and Sam would have been happy if she hadn't just figured out the source of the problem.

Wearing a gaudy green Western shirt and a cowboy hat as big as the hubcap on his Cadillac, Linc Slocum had shown up for adoption day at Willow Springs Wild Horse Center and he wasn't a bit pleased to find he wasn't welcome.

Chapter Fifteen ❧

"I thought you weren't workin' today," Linc snapped at Brynna.

Chills ran down Sam's neck and arms. How had Linc found out? Even Dad didn't know.

"I'm not," Brynna said, smiling. "But Mr. Black is my boss, and he's privy to all my records." Then she corrected herself, "BLM's records."

"I don't care what he's *privy* to," Linc blustered. "I came here lookin' to get a horse."

Hugh stood beside Mr. Black. Under his breath, Hugh—who Sam had always thought of as Bale-Tosser, because the first time she'd seen him at Willow Springs, he'd been feeding the captive mustangs—said something that made Mr. Black's eyebrows arch high on his forehead.

"Mr. Slocum," Rex said, "maybe you'd like to step inside the office for a minute."

"No, sir," Linc said. "That's not necessary. I'm a citizen of these parts, and all these good people are my neighbors."

When Linc spread his arms to include those gathered for adoption day, Sam couldn't help but scan the crowd. She'd only recognized a few people all morning.

"Suit yourself." Rex paused for a second, glanced back at Hugh, then said in a disbelieving tone, "It's my understanding that you're suspected of some prohibited acts involving wild horses. Acts requiring a two-thousand-dollar fine for each violation?"

Hugh recited the charges, "Harassment—several counts of that—negligence, and maybe even an attempt to destroy—"

"None of that was ever proven!" Linc interrupted. His face swelled like a red balloon, overinflated and ready to pop. He took a quick look around, noticed a crowd gathering, and gave up.

"Besides, I don't know what all the fuss is about. I'm not adopting one of these broomtails. I'm here to see if BLM's rounded up my Appy mare Hotspot."

"We have a brand inspector on site to protect against such possibilities," Rex Black assured him.

"She's out there runnin' loose somewhere. Not that I'd blame you for bringing her in. I'd give BLM the benefit of the doubt. Accidents do happen, you know."

Sam glimpsed Linc's glare at Brynna as if the capture of the Phantom and the injuries that had followed could have been accidental.

Yeah right, Sam thought. He'd had the horse roped from the back of a moving truck, then tied, terrified and struggling, to an immovable barrel of concrete. How could that be accidental?

Though Rex had been willing to let Linc off the hook, Brynna crossed her arms and pretended to meditate a few seconds.

Then, frowning, she said, "Linc, if you've knowingly allowed a domestic horse to run free on public lands without paying a use fee—" She glanced at her boss. "What do you think, Rex? Doesn't that warrant a fine?"

With forced patience, Rex said, "I think as long as he's just here to watch the adoptions, we'll worry about that later."

For once, Linc Slocum was smart enough to spot a way out and take it.

Though a rustle of interest followed Linc as he stomped through the crowd, Sam didn't stare after him.

That's why she noticed Rex beckon her stepmother closer and heard him mutter, "Back off, Brynna. You're on leave. Act like it. Keep this up and you'll compromise your own adoption."

Sam wasn't sure what he meant, but Brynna understood.

Looking sheepish, she said, "Thanks, boss."

Then she turned and her eyes widened. When Sam looked, too, it was just in time to see Dad riding up.

Had he heard Rex's comment about Brynna's adoption?

Brynna hurried through the throng of people, trying to get as far from Rex as she could so that Dad didn't question anything that was going on.

Before she reached Dad, though, Linc Slocum spotted him. Even though Linc was a total jerk, he idolized Dad. He saw Wyatt Forster as a true Westerner, everything he wanted to be. Linc never let a chance go by to show others that they were acquainted.

"Hey there, neighbor," Linc shouted. "You're looking mighty fine today, just struttin' like a turkey gobbler with that pretty scarf of yours."

Sam's hands clamped on her reins. She could hear a screech in her brain telling Linc Slocum to keep his eyes off the wild rag she'd made for her dad, but she managed to stay silent.

Dad touched the brim of his hat in greeting, but he didn't say a word. He simply rode on and stopped next to Brynna.

"Can I show you something in that far corral?" Dad asked.

Rex had just announced that names would be

drawn and adopters would be given the chance to bid for horses in ten minutes, so Brynna and Dad hurried off.

Sam halted Ace nearby as her parents considered the Spanish Mustang.

"You might wanna keep your eye on that gelding," Dad said, pointing at the very horse he'd be getting for his birthday.

"How come?" Brynna asked.

Sam admired Brynna's casual tone, but more than that, she was astounded that Brynna had known Dad and the mustang belonged together. There were hundreds of horses here, and Dad had gravitated to only one.

"At first, I thought he was kinda rank. You know, a mean son of a gun, charging the fence when people got too close, then backing off, shaking his head. But then I noticed he only did it with men. Never women or kids.

"So, I thought, okay, he's been hurt by a man. But then he started limping. When I went in to check him, though, he galloped away, leavin' me with a mouthful of dust. Have you seen him move?"

Brynna nodded, but Dad wasn't done telling about the mustang's tricks.

"I watched him pull the buckskin's tail, and when the horse whirled around to face him, he just stood there, looking innocent." Dad stopped to take a breath. Then he shook his head in disbelief. "The horse knows about joshing."

"We've noticed him," Brynna admitted. "He's a tough little guy. Even when he was first brought in, he stayed calm. Considering the heat and stress, he did better than the other adult horses. He was wet, but not lathered."

"Nice coloring, too," Dad said as the gelding turned and sun glinted on his pearly neck.

"In the paperwork we described him as a blue roan paint, but that doesn't do him justice, does it?"

Dad didn't answer. He took one hand from Popcorn's reins and rubbed the back of his neck. Sam knew Dad was fretting because he'd admired the mustang too openly.

A microphone screeched and Rex Black's voice announced it was time for the wild horse lottery.

"Gotta go," Brynna said.

Before Dad started after her, he looked at Sam and asked, "You don't think he's too flashy?"

"Pepper says there's no bad color for a good horse," Sam told him.

Dad shook his head and exhaled. "He might be right, at that."

Sam couldn't make herself watch the lottery. She didn't want to know if someone else had placed a higher bid on the Spanish Mustang, because she knew Brynna couldn't bid much more than the $200 she already had.

No, Sam planned to stay right here with the small, uppity, almost-last-of-his-kind Spanish Mustang that had charmed Dad.

If Brynna came back and announced the gelding was a new member of their family, then she'd get excited.

"So, you won't even let me get to know you?" she called as the horse crowded in with his company of older geldings.

She couldn't see him very well, and she began wondering about the other horses in there. Would any of them get new homes?

The buckskin and the grays might.

Brynna had told her that most of the horses that went unadopted were small bays. Regardless of age or conformation, people liked brightly colored horses, and they were the first to be chosen.

Not fair, Sam thought, but maybe she was biased because she was short with reddish-brown hair, herself.

Sam was glad when Hugh asked her to help him load horses for the adopters. He took her over to the chutes and explained that horses over one year old must be loaded into livestock trailers and only weanlings could go in two-horse trailers.

It became her job to verify this fact with smiling people who walked up brandishing their signed care agreements, ready to take their horses home. So far, everyone had read the fine print, and she hadn't had to tell a single person they had to come back with a different vehicle.

Most of the horses loaded well, but they were nervous and hot. They'd drunk so much water in their corrals, Sam could hear swishing in their bellies as they sprinted past her side of the chute, into the trailer, bound for homes they'd never dreamed of.

Almost an hour later, she found out the Spanish Mustang was coming home to River Bend Ranch.

"Looks like I really walked into ambush this time."

Sam turned, smiling at the sound of Dad's voice, but he didn't look happy.

He'd been joking, right? She gazed into his face, but she couldn't tell.

Was he excited? Irritated? Resigned to accepting the horse because it was, after all, a present?

Her only clue was Popcorn. Dad was leading the horse, but Popcorn hung back at the end of his reins, rolling his blue eyes and tossing his head up so that Sam could see his milky throat.

"Do you like him, Dad?" Sam asked. "I know you do."

Dad's face stayed blank as he said, "We're gonna need another mount for the cattle drive, what with Amigo retiring and Strawberry goin' lame. Might as well be him."

Sam took a deep breath and let it out.

Might as well be him. That wasn't exactly a decla-ration of love, but she guessed it could be worse.

"What I came to tell ya, though, is there are things to do at home. I'll trailer Ace and Popcorn back, and you and Brynna will come along with the new horse later." Dad must have felt Hugh staring at him, because he looked up. He gave the other man a grate-ful nod. "Thanks for everything you do to back her up," Dad said, gesturing toward Brynna's office. "I swear, that woman does not know when she's beat."

Did Dad mean *beat*, like really tired? Or did he mean *beaten*, like she'd lost? Sam didn't ask Dad before he left, because she didn't want to know.

Chapter Sixteen ১৯

They didn't put the Spanish Mustang in the ten-acre pasture right away, although Sam had a feeling he would have done fine. They put him in the same portable pen adjoining the pasture that they'd used for Penny and other horses.

Head low in a herding motion, the gelding acted like a wild stallion, telling the other horses he was the boss and as soon as he could get on their side of the fence, he'd prove it.

Dad was polite at dinner. He blew out the candles on his chocolate cake with buttercream frosting and thanked everyone for his gifts. He was so mannerly and stiff, in fact, that Sam didn't know how Brynna stayed calm.

Finally, when Dad went out to explain the new

horse to Dallas, walking right past the portable pen with the mustang gazing after him, Sam asked her, "Why aren't you crying your eyes out?"

"He'll come around," Brynna said. Then, with a little less confidence, she called to Gram, "You think so, don't you, Grace?"

"I'm sure of it," Gram said. "Did you see the way he sat forward in his chair, elbows on the table, too, I might add, when you were telling about the stock that horse came from, and the way he chimed in, knowing all he did about Good Thunder Meadows?"

Gram was right, Sam thought. Dad had heard that an ex-cavalryman had lived all alone in that high mountain valley, and when a severe winter left the Indians who were his neighbors starving, he'd used his rifle to bring down game for food. They'd named the sound of his big gun "good thunder" for the bounty it brought.

"Oh, something else interesting I heard from Lila today, when I called to see how Jen's doing," Gram said. "Can you believe that a tourist from Ontario, Canada, stopped in at Sheriff Ballard's office to report a white-faced bull charged his car out by Highway 34?" Gram looked meaningfully at Sam.

"That has to be the same bull that hurt Jen," Sam said.

"Of course that's what they think," Gram said. "Those Hazard bloodlines have always been risky. But Jed's gone out looking for the beast and can't seem to find him at Fishbait Springs where he used to be."

"Good," Sam said. She was sorry about the tourist from Ontario, but she was glad the bull had deserted his Fishbait Springs territory, especially if it was the Phantom's territory as well.

It was barely light the next morning when Sam heard the Spanish Mustang squeal. She sat up in bed and listened as hooves pounded to a background of men's voices.

They couldn't be gentling him already, Sam thought as she pulled on jeans and a sweatshirt. Even though the horse had been at Willow Springs for a long time and wasn't totally wild, he needed a few days to settle in, didn't he?

Sam ran down the stairs so fast, she almost missed the last one.

When she got to the round pen, she saw that Dad was letting Pepper and Dallas break the Spanish Mustang to saddle. Not gentle — break.

"Why are you letting them do that?" Sam asked.

Clinging like a monkey, Pepper was wrestling the mustang into a halter.

"Calm down, honey," Dad said. "If he's going to be of any use during the fall drive, we've got to hurry him along a little."

"Hurry him along?" Sam cried. "He's hurting him."

"If he's a River Bend horse, the River Bend foreman can decide how to bring him around," Dad said.

"Is this because we didn't ask you first? Because he's wild?"

"Sam," Dad said in a cautioning tone.

"I don't care if I get in trouble," she said. "Pepper's heavy. He's hanging on his neck! What if—"

"Sam," Dad said again, but this time his tone was gentle. "Most of the horses on this ranch, including Ace, were bucked out this way. Haltered, saddled, then ridden to a standstill. And Ace is a good horse, isn't he?"

"You know I think so, but this isn't the old days! You don't have to do it like that!"

Even though the mustang's sounds were squalls of anger, not pain, Sam couldn't stand to listen. But she wouldn't go back and hide in the house, either. That would be like deserting him.

She covered her ears and stared at the horse. He kept bucking, even when he was haltered and Pepper was walking away.

Dad pulled her hands down from her ears and made her face him.

"Sam, have you known me to be cruel to any animal? Ever?"

Sam was shaking her head when Pepper and Dallas walked up. Brushing his chili pepper red hair back from his eyes, Pepper looked torn. He was excited by the prospect of riding a wild horse, but he liked Sam. She could see he didn't want her mad at him. Still, she glared at him, just so he'd know how she felt.

"He told us—your dad did—if the going gets too rough and we think we're goin' to hurt ourselves or the horse, to bail off," Pepper said.

"Not that it makes a whole lotta sense," Dallas said, "but Wyatt and I have worked out a truce on this. Even though his way makes it harder in the long run, I'm willin' to go along. Don't want my rough rider"—Dallas paused to jerk a thumb toward Pepper—"to get hurt. But I still say, if ya let one of these critters get it in his *loco* head that all he has to do is make it hard on ya, and you'll bail—why, every time that happens, you can multiply your breakin' time by five."

"Days?" Sam asked.

Five days seemed like a short time to train a horse to carry a rider, but then Dallas gave her a scoffing look and said, "Hours."

"Go get dressed for church," Dad told her.

"You're just trying to get rid of me," Sam argued.

"I'm not. You don't even have to eat breakfast if you don't want, but your Gram will have my hide if I make you late for church. Go get dressed and then come back down. You can watch until they're backing the car out to leave."

Sam stared into Dad's brown eyes. He was telling her the truth.

"Okay, but you have no idea how fast I can get dressed," she told him, and then she ran.

Her hair was clean and so was the yellow sundress Gram had ironed for her last night. It hung on her bedroom door, ready to wear with her white sandals. Sam pulled on the dress, slipped on the sandals, then bent at the waist, ran the brush through her hair four times, and flipped her head back. She didn't take the time to look in the mirror. She looked good enough. Church wasn't where she went to show off.

She grabbed her purse and ran back down the stairs, ignoring Gram's plea to know what in the *world* was going on.

When Sam reached the corral, the Spanish Mustang was saddled.

They'd slapped a saddle on him and hidden his wings, Sam thought.

And he wore a halter with two dangling rope reins.

"That halter looks tight," Sam told Dad as she came to stand beside him.

"It's snug," Dad agreed, "and the reins are cut so that he can't get a hoof through one or the other of 'em and hurt himself."

That made sense, but Sam didn't like the way Dallas was holding the horse so still.

Then she realized it wasn't Dallas's doing. The blue-and-white pinto snorted through wide nostrils, but he seemed almost calm. His eyes were fixed on Dad, even though Pepper was approaching him.

"He's watching you, Dad," Sam said.

Dad didn't answer, but Sam kept staring. Even though Pepper was close enough to touch the horse, his ears flicked toward Dad.

"Okay, now Pepper will cheek him, just grab

the cheek piece of the halter," Dad explained, "and then . . ."

Sam held her breath as the horse spun away from the grip that was so close to his eye.

"And then," Dad repeated when Pepper didn't lose his hold on the halter, "he'll wait for a good place to launch himself up into the saddle, and—there!"

Pepper had barely hit the saddle when Dallas released his hold on the horse.

The Spanish Mustang immediately tried to get his head down to buck, but Pepper kept hold of the cheek strap as well as the reins.

A squeal of insult erupted from the mustang and he began bucking and spinning in circles. His long tail was tucked tight, so he wouldn't trip, but the arch of Pepper's body didn't change. Sam didn't admire Pepper a bit, but she didn't know how he could hold the reins and the cheek piece and still stay centered on the mustang's back.

"He's showin' off, but he's not serious about this," Dad said slowly. "I wonder what he's got in mind."

The mustang looked serious enough to Sam, but she didn't feel sorry for Pepper. He'd be aching in lots of new places tonight, and it would serve him right.

Just then, the Spanish Mustang stopped. He shifted his weight from hoof to hoof as if he'd just figured out that Pepper was off balance while he was clinging to the cheek piece.

He gave a low neigh.

"I swear that animal just said, 'aha,'" Dad muttered, and then the mustang lunged.

First he lunged left, toward the hand Pepper used to hold the cheek piece, but Pepper felt the horse shift and let go in time to clap his legs tight around the mustang's middle.

The horse jumped right, gave a couple of hops, and even Sam could tell he wasn't serious now.

"Some of 'em, that's all they ever do," Dad said, but he didn't sound convinced that the Spanish Mustang was one of them.

"Don't let him get his head down," Dallas shouted as the gelding's ears pricked forward.

But he didn't buck. He shook all over like a big dog. Then he slipped into his beautiful running walk.

Like a Spanish Paso Fino, he circled the corral with elegance.

"Uh-uh," Dad said. "He's not done." Dad shook his head, then shouted, "Keep those reins tight."

They watched as the minutes ticked off, but Dad still didn't think the horse had given in.

"He's a thinker," Dad said grimly. "I'll give him—"

And then the Spanish Mustang was charging. With all the strength in his powerful hind legs, he flew out of his graceful gait and toward the fence.

Chapter Seventeen ❧

$\mathcal{P}$epper let himself fall off, but he hit the ground rolling.

He was smiling when he stood up and brushed himself off.

"He's too pretty," Pepper said. "I don't want to scuff him up."

"Too bad he doesn't feel the same about you," Sam shouted as the mustang galloped past, kicking, and jolted his shoulder against Pepper's.

The blue-roan pinto was hard to catch, and finally, Dallas had to rope him, but this time the horse skipped the hopping and the running walk. Without giving Pepper time to settle in, he catapulted himself upright, pawing toward the sun, then ducked down so hard Pepper had no hope of keeping the horse's head up.

"He's practically standing on his head," Dad muttered beside her, and then Sam saw the mustang's muscles gather. He slammed back onto his hind legs, and before he reached for the sky again, Pepper fell off.

The mustang saved his energy. He stood still, watching Pepper.

"Need a hand?" Dallas called out.

"No," Pepper said, and though the word sounded like a groan, Pepper stood, retrieved his hat, and dusted it off like a rodeo rider.

He didn't turn his back on the horse. In fact, all four of them, plus Gram and Brynna from inside the house, were watching the Spanish Mustang as he trotted toward the fence.

Wet but not lathered from his efforts, he stopped, stood with forefeet braced apart, and lowered his head so he could glare through his forelock at Dad.

This time Dad couldn't deny the horse was watching him, but that didn't mean he felt like bonding with him.

"You're not my horse," he said in a normal, conversational tone. "You're the property of the federal government for a whole long year, and after that, you belong to the River Bend Ranch, so don't put your attitude on with me."

Dallas and Pepper laughed, but Sam was quiet.

Did he know he was Dad's horse, or had the Spanish Mustang tagged Dad as the most threatening stallion, the challenger who had to be tested?

"I'm gonna try him again, 'kay, Wyatt?" Pepper said.

"Go ahead," Dad told him.

The horse let Dallas come and hold his halter, but when Pepper got close to the horse and grabbed the cheek piece, the blue-roan pinto planted a hoof on the cowboy's right boot toe and refused to move.

"Ow! Ow, get off!" Pepper shouted.

Both men pushed at the gelding's shoulder, and though he swayed against their strength, he didn't move until Dallas released his halter.

Swinging his head and the two-rope reins, he circled the corral three times at his beautiful running walk.

"This time, you're not buckin' me off!" Pepper shouted, but when he started to stalk toward the horse, Dad called out.

"No more."

"But, Wyatt—"

"Nope, don't even ask. You're getting mad, and that's no way to train a horse."

Pepper couldn't deny it. He stood with his hands on his hips, watching the horse watch him.

"And I need you all in one piece so you can do some work around here," Dallas said. "Don't want to be dragging you outta there by your armpits."

Just when Sam had started to relax and feel better about going to church, Dallas narrowed his eyes toward Dad and said, "You're not just going to let him off, are you?"

It took Sam a minute to realize Dallas was talking about the horse.

"No," Dad said quietly.

"Sam, let's go," Brynna said as she bustled out of the house.

"No, please," Sam begged, but both Gram and Brynna were watching Dad. "I go to church all the time, can I please stay and watch, Dad?"

Dallas mumbled that Sam would do as much praying watching this horse as she would in church, but he had the good sense not to say it too loud.

Still, Gram heard, and tsked her tongue. "Samantha, didn't you promise Ally you'd help with the Cherubs?"

Sam moaned. How hard could it be to line up a bunch of little kids to go sing? But she *had* promised, and Ally was counting on her.

"We're stopping to see Jen, too," Brynna said, and Sam wanted to scream in frustration. More than anything in the world, she wanted to see Jen, but who'd look after this horse?

She pounded her fists against the sides of her thighs, and if that looked weird while she was wearing a sundress, she really didn't care.

"Okay," Sam said finally, and started toward Gram's car.

Behind her, she heard Gram talking to Dad.

"It would do you some good to come to church with us once in a while, Wyatt."

When Dad didn't answer right away, Sam looked back to see Dad gazing up in the sky.

"Wyatt?" Gram repeated.

"Remember before the church in Darton was built?" Dad asked. "Remember what you used to tell folks who didn't know how we got along without one?"

"Of course I do," Gram said. "I understand. But do you have any messages you want me to give anyone at church, since you almost never leave this ranch?"

It was quiet for a few seconds, but then Dad cleared his throat.

"Yeah," he said. "If you see Jed Kenworthy, you might mention Ross is out looking for that renegade bull of his. And then ask if he's quit bein' so danged hardheaded."

In the car, Sam stared over her shoulder until she couldn't see the ranch anymore, and then she asked, "What did you used to say, Gram? About there being no church out here?"

"I said that the sky was the roof of my cathedral and the desert was its floor and any time I paid attention, I could feel a higher power all around me."

"Oh," Sam said, and then she decided it would be okay to say a prayer that Dad and the Spanish Mustang didn't hurt each other.

❊ ❊ ❊

Forty minutes later, Sam had discovered she had a bit of skill with children.

Her fingers tied a presentable bow in a bedraggled dress sash that had been slammed in a car door and dragged all the way to church. She found a little boy's clip-on bow tie in his jubilant friend's pocket and wiped milk mustaches from two small faces.

Those were victories, sort of, but Sam had also wiped way too many noses.

When she returned to the sanctuary and sat down next to Gram, Sam couldn't help glancing over at the swelling front of Brynna's dress and hoping Brynna and Dad would take care of all the gross parts of child-rearing themselves.

"You're really pretty good at this," Ally said after church. She grinned, but she had faint shadows under her eyes as if she hadn't slept much.

"Thanks, but putting them in a straight line so they can march up to the altar is nothing compared to what you do once they get there," Sam said. "They sounded really good. And you have an incredible voice."

"I should sing more quietly and just accompany them on my guitar, but they insist they have to hear me," Ally said. "And I don't mind performing."

Sam sighed. "Then we're lucky we'll have you, at least, for the talent show."

"Come on, you like being up in front of an audience

a little bit, don't you?" Ally asked.

"I like photography and writing," Sam pointed out. "Neither of those is a performance art."

"And horseback riding," Ally said. "Everyone knows you like that."

"Also not a performance art. At least, not the way I do it."

Ally laughed, but then she looked worried. "What if we don't have enough people for the talent show and Mr. Blair says you have to do something?"

"Unless he says my grade depends on it, there's no way," Sam said, and she meant it.

Jen was asleep when they got to the hospital. The nurse said she'd had a restless night, run a fever, and wasn't allowed any visitors.

"Is that supposed to happen?" Sam asked.

The nurse hesitated. "I don't suppose you're all family?"

"No, but I'm her best friend," Sam said.

Apparently that was good enough to receive such minor information, because the nurse smiled as she touched Sam's arm and said, "It's not unusual, dear. I'll help her call you when she wakes up."

Two days later, Jen still hadn't called.

A lot of other things had happened. Sam had called a bunch of people who refused to be in the talent show, for instance, and Pepper and Dallas had divided their long days between stacking hay and trying to break the Spanish Mustang to saddle.

The blue-and-white gelding refused to give in. Tireless and tricky, he unseated Pepper with new bucks every time.

On the second night, Sam couldn't sleep.

She stood at her window, staring at the black sky and silver stars, worrying about Jen.

Her friend's mom had called and told Sam that Jen was doing better, but if she was better, why hadn't she phoned herself? It was totally out of character, and she knew something was wrong.

A crunch of dirt drew Sam's attention to the sound of the unhappy horse in the corral below. She couldn't see him from here, but she heard the mustang, painted with wings, trapped and trotting in circles.

With his fluid gait, he patrolled his tiny corral as he must have patrolled his herd in the wild, trotting around and around, keeping them together and safe.

The Spanish Mustang wasn't the only restless one.

Blaze gave a sad, warbling howl. He sounded like a wild thing rather than a domesticated dog, and the sound gave Sam chills.

"What on earth is wrong with that dog?" Gram called from her room.

It sounded as if Blaze sat on the front porch. Sam hoped so. She wasn't annoyed. She was scared.

Blaze had his secrets and there was no way he

could tell her, but she was afraid he'd disappear like he had early in the summer. Though it was still August, adventuring into the wild now could be dangerous. Overnight, temperatures could drop to freezing.

What if he swam across the river and then his wet fur froze?

"I'll go bring him in," Sam called down the dark hallway to Gram and whoever else had been wakened by the dog.

Downstairs, Sam opened the kitchen door. Blaze wasn't on the porch.

"Blaze!" she shouted. A cold wind whipped her voice away and she yelled more loudly. "Blaze, come!"

Nice, she told herself. *I'd sure want to answer someone snarling at me like that.*

With a sweet voice and a dog cookie from the box in the pantry, Sam tried again.

"Blaze, come here, good boy."

Even though she turned on the porch light, it took minutes of staring into the night before she saw him. Walking slowly and reluctantly, Blaze came from the direction of the bridge. He wasn't wet, but he whined, pacing back and forth a few yards away, sliding beseeching eyes her way.

"Sorry, boy, but you have to come in." She held a cookie up so he could see it.

Blaze hopped up on the wooden porch, but he didn't come inside.

Should she grab his collar while he pretended to sniff the boards as if he hadn't smelled them a thousand times before? She would, but he stayed just out of reach and she was afraid if she lunged, he'd take off for real.

"You're stalling," Sam told the dog gently as she just stood there, holding the screen door open.

At last, Blaze shook all over, making the dog tags on his collar jingle. Then he came inside, turned in three restless circles, and flopped down. With a sigh, he rested his head on his paws with an uneaten dog cookie between them.

Since Blaze was locked safe inside the house, Sam should have been able to sleep. That's what she told herself as she climbed the stairs to her bedroom, but her arms still had goose bumps.

"And it's just wrong," Sam told Cougar as she pulled her covers into a nest that included the cat. "We shouldn't be able to just dive into a peaceful night's sleep when that horse is so unhappy, and tomorrow I'm going to do something about it."

The next morning, Sam woke up thinking about her vow. She dressed hurriedly. Dad was not going to leave home for work on the range before she had a talk with him.

Brown sugar and cinnamon wafted up the stairs as she came down. Gram had already made a batch of oatmeal cookies and the delicious smell made Sam consider a detour.

Gram was taking two plump cookies from a cooling rack. She wrapped a paper napkin around them and handed the warm bundle to Sam.

"Thanks."

"You're welcome," Gram said, "but they're not for you. They're for the new horse. Brynna says he likes them, so go on and see if he'll take them."

Gram tried to sound gruff, but her kindness shone through.

"I bet he won't," Sam said. "They're all three — Dallas, Pepper, and Dad — teaching him all the wrong things about people. Gram, I can't stand it."

"You won't have to," Gram said. "We're going to Darton. We'll make a quick stop to talk with Jen and — " Gram held up her index finger before Sam could remind her of their Sunday trip. "This time, we won't take no for an answer. Lila says she's well enough for company and we'll see her and ask her what she needs for school. Then we're doing your school shopping."

Sam had never really liked shopping, but she'd go, right after she faced Dad. She'd just caught a glimpse of him in the barn and that meant she had him cornered.

As she walked out to the corral and unwrapped the warm oatmeal cookies, she noticed they weren't studded with raisins as they usually were.

Brynna must have told Gram the same thing she had Sam. When he came to raisins in oatmeal cookies, the little horse just spit them out.

"Here you go, just the way you like them."

A swish of a flaxen tail was all Sam got in return. Brynna had called the mustang catlike, and he was. Until Sam looked away, pretending she didn't care if he came to her, the horse stood across the small corral and ignored her.

He needed a name. And he was dirty, Sam realized.

On Saturday, Brynna had told Inez that once the wild horses settled in, they kept themselves pretty clean with dust baths. This one hadn't settled in. He wasn't about to roll on his back, making himself vulnerable in a place of strange corrals and rough humans.

Oh yeah, she was going to have a talk with Dad, all right. At least that's what she thought until Gram, dressed in a navy blue skirt and a crisp white blouse and no apron, went striding across the ranch yard to the barn.

Despite her curiosity, Sam waited outside. Gram could probably accomplish more than she could.

Besides, the Spanish Mustang was wandering in her direction. Nostrils fluttering, he came to the fence for his cookie, but he was wary. He grabbed the cookie and bolted off a step to chew it.

When the gelding's hooves were still, she heard Dad's voice.

"I know it! All they're doing is teaching him he can't be rode."

Yeah, Sam thought. At least Dad understood.

But that didn't seem to be good enough for Gram. Her voice cut across Dad's.

"That horse is goin' downhill. Stop being stubborn, Wyatt, and just . . ."

Sam couldn't hear the rest, but a minute later, the Spanish Mustang dashed away as Dad walked up to stand beside her.

"I guess you heard your gram," Dad said.

"A little," Sam admitted.

"You know what Ross said?" Dad asked her, and when Sam shook her head no, he told her. "Said that horse is thinking about turning into a biter. Ross said now when Pepper comes up to cheek him, his eyes narrow, ears flatten, and his lips draw back from his teeth."

Dad sighed.

Sam bit her lip to keep from saying a thing. Dad was headed in the right direction and anything she said might derail him. But it was so hard waiting.

Dad squinted through the haze of dust the horse had left behind. Then he said, "Guess it's my turn."

Chapter Eighteen ⟊

Gram let Sam off in front of the hospital while she looked for a parking place.

From their stop at the hospital on Sunday, Sam remembered the right elevator. She got off on the right floor, too. This time she didn't ask for permission, just counted the doors and watched the room numbers until she reached Jen's. Then she slipped inside.

Nearly as pale as her white-blond braids, Jen leaned back against pillows, staring listlessly at the wall-mounted television.

"Hey," Sam whispered.

The first thing Jen did was clap when she saw Sam come through the door of her room.

"I'm so bored," Jen said, but she also winced, leaning toward the pain in her side.

"Hurt?" Sam asked, and it was as if she'd given Jen permission to be honest.

"Ow, ow, ow," Jen said, and though she smiled as she said it, Sam could tell she meant it. Once she caught her breath, Jen gestured at a clear vase of yellow roses. Their stems jutted straight up from the water, but their soft, petaled heads were bent. "My flowers are dying, but they were really cool at first."

"Yeah? Well you're the only person I know who ever got any, so don't expect me to feel sorry for you," Sam said. She crossed her arms as if she were jealous, but the truth was, Sam did feel sorry for Jen. She looked miserable.

Jen sighed and that seemed to hurt, too. Then she nodded toward the tray pulled up next to her bed. It held a box of tissues, a plastic cup and pitcher, a book, some magazines, and a tablet of lavender paper.

"Mom brought me the paper and told me to make a list of things I'd need before I went back to school," Jen said matter-of-factly. "And then Dad said I'm not going back to school."

"Oh no," Sam moaned. "I hope your mom wins."

"Me too, because he's being completely illogical. And wrong."

Sam heard the squeak of Gram's rubber-soled shoes at the door.

"Hello, Jennifer," Gram said as she came to stand

beside her. With one wrinkled hand, Gram brushed a stray lock of Jen's hair back from her forehead. "How are you, honey? You're looking a little peaked."

When Jen shook her head silently, unable to speak and hold back tears at the same time, Gram dropped a kiss on the top of her head.

Sam scolded herself, remembering how she'd thought Gram cared more about Mrs. Allen's flies than Jen's injury. How dumb could she be?

"There's her list," Sam said, pointing.

Gram scanned it quickly, promised to pick her up a tee-shirt in one of the bright colors Jen liked, and a minute later they were out of the room, making way for Jen's parents.

Though they walked side by side, Lila and Jed Kenworthy looked really separate. Forced to explain to someone else, Sam couldn't have, but she'd seen them at odds before and today was no different. Even Gram didn't try to have a conversation with them. She just waved and headed for an open elevator.

Shopping was okay. Sam picked out a tee-shirt the color of mango sherbet for Jen, and one the shade of lime sherbet for herself. It was a lot brighter than anything she'd usually wear, but Sam figured if one vivid tee-shirt helped Jen cheer up, two would finish the job.

They decided to drop off the things they'd bought

for Jen later. Gram was as eager to get back to the ranch and see if Dad had made progress with the mustang as Sam was. And Gram had barely parked her yellow Buick when Brynna pulled her BLM truck in behind them.

It only took a glance inside the round pen to see that Dad and the mustang were exhausted.

"Never seen such a stubborn critter," Dad said through the rails to all three of them, but only Sam climbed up high enough to look down on him.

The mustang had been stripped of halter and saddle, and though his blue wing markings showed again, their pearly background had sweat-darkened to gray. He faced determinedly away from Dad, as if staring through a knothole in a fence board.

Dad looked relaxed as he leaned against his own side of the corral, but his face was beaded with sweat and his brow was smeared with dirt that had turned to something that looked a lot like mud.

"He knows that if he's not paying attention to me, I'm going to keep running him around, but he *will not* let me win."

Sam knew how this horse and human game went. Jake had taught it to her, and she'd used it with the Phantom and Dark Sunshine.

Dad tossed his riata toward the mustang, with no intention of lassoing him, and the horse took off galloping around the pen. He glanced back at the rope, and once it lay dead and still in the dirt, he slowed to a trot, then stopped.

Dad jerked the rope back, stepped out in front of the horse, and did it again. He kept throwing the rope and controlling the horse's direction of travel.

From doing it herself, Sam knew that Dad was studying the horse's ears, eyes, and muscles, anticipating what the horse wanted to do, then tossing the rope and making it seem like his own idea.

Snorting and pawing, tossing his flaxen forelock away from impatient eyes, the mustang couldn't seem to figure out why he wasn't in control. Even when he turned away from Dad, he kept one ear cocked toward him.

Since they were both breathing hard, Dad let the horse have a break.

As if she'd been watching from inside the house, Brynna eased past the screen door and walked out in bare feet to stand beside Sam. If Dad noticed his audience had grown, he gave no sign. All of his attention was fixed on the mustang.

After about five minutes, Dad clucked his tongue. The mustang tensed, but he refused to turn his body. Once more he snorted, and this time his hoof struck out at the fence. Then his head turned to see what Dad was doing.

Sam almost laughed aloud when Dad moved a step to his left so that the horse could barely see him, even though his eyes were set on the sides of his head.

With another step left, Dad ended up directly

behind the horse. But as Dad had said, the mustang was a "thinker" and he'd figured out what Dad was doing. He stamped and moved up so close to the fence, his chest pressed against it.

But Dad had faced more stubborn horses than the mustang had men, and he understood their curiosity.

Dad scuffed his toe in the dirt. The horse's skin shivered. He wanted to know what was happening, but he didn't want to give Dad the satisfaction of forcing him to turn and look.

It was so quiet, Sam could hear Brynna breathing beside her. The only other sound was Dad, scuffing the sole of his boot against the grainy corral floor.

Then he stopped, and the mustang's skin shivered once more.

When Dad made that double-cluck again, the horse swung around to face him. Trembling with curiosity and weariness, the gelding studied this confusing human, and for the first time, Dad talked to him.

"Hey, Blue," Dad said.

Brynna reached over to squeeze Sam's hand as the horse stretched out his nose. He flared his nostrils to take in Dad's smell, but he still didn't touch him.

Dad remained still for what seemed like an hour; then the horse nuzzled his shirt.

That lasted for a few seconds, and then the horse startled away. Sam didn't know if Dad had breathed more deeply, or the horse had caught his eye movement, or if maybe the horse had frightened himself, but he only went a few steps.

And then, just when Sam thought the mustang might be about to start the entire game over again, Dad walked away.

This was the test.

Sam knew it, but the headstrong little horse, once king of his own world, didn't, because when Dad walked away, just like Dark Sunshine and the Phantom before him, the Spanish Mustang followed.

Sam rushed inside to call Jen. She'd only told her friend a little about Dad's new horse, but she knew Jen would appreciate how cool this was.

The phone had only rung once when a male voice said, "Hello?"

Had she asked for the wrong hospital room?

Then she recognized the lightly accented voice. It belonged to Ryan Slocum.

"Hi, this is Sam," she said, and when nothing happened, she added, "I'd like to talk with Jen, please."

"I'm sorry," Ryan said. "She's just had some tests and—"

"I'm fine."

Sam heard Jen's voice not too far from the telephone. But her tone wasn't insistent. She sounded almost pouty.

"She's really not," Ryan said quietly, and Sam knew that this time he was right.

Worry clamped Sam like the jaws of some giant

insect. Why wasn't Jen getting better instead of worse?

"Tell her I love her," Sam insisted.

When Ryan didn't respond, Sam didn't let him off the hook. "You have to tell her."

"Yes, I know." Ryan sounded annoyed. "I'm to 'cowboy up' regardless of what it costs in embarrassment."

"That's right," Sam said.

She heard Ryan clear his throat, take a deep breath, then blurt, "Jennifer, Samantha says to tell you that she loves you and, I assume, that you're to get well quickly so that we don't ever have to do this again."

"Tell her she's a wimp," Jen responded weakly, but Sam could hear the smile in her best friend's voice.

"Samantha?" Ryan said stiffly. "Next time you're thinking ill of me, I hope you stop and remember this. Ask yourself if Jake Ely would have done what I did just now."

Sam didn't hesitate.

Jake would rather let his tongue swell up in his mouth until he choked on it than transmit a message of loving friendship.

"He wouldn't," Sam agreed. "But you didn't do it for me. You did it for Jen."

"Precisely," Ryan said.

When he gently hung up on her, Sam still didn't know what he meant.

Chapter Nineteen ❧

The next morning, Sam had finished gathering eggs in a wicker basket when she detoured toward the round corral.

The Spanish Mustang was awfully quiet. Was he exhausted from yesterday's standoff with Dad?

A quick glance between the fence rails showed her no horse.

"What?" Sam gasped. An egg rolled out of the basket and splatted near her boots. She set the basket on the ground and was about to climb up the fence for a better look when she noticed what she should have seen in the first place. The gate was open.

Stepping around Blaze, who'd appeared to lap up the broken egg, Sam hurried toward the house.

"Hey, the Spanish Mustang is gone!" she called before she was even inside.

"If by 'hey' you mean, 'Grandmother,'" Gram said patiently, "I know. I held the gate open for him at four-thirty this morning."

"Dad's riding him?" Sam gasped. "Already? I wanted to watch!"

She turned as the door into the living room opened and Brynna, still in her nightgown and slippers, came yawning into the kitchen.

"You would've needed a flashlight," Brynna said. "It was still dark outside. He rolled out of bed at three-thirty A.M."

And he'd ridden the mustang out of the corral an hour later.

Sam couldn't believe it. She looked from Brynna's face to Gram's, then glanced at the kitchen clock. It was nearly seven o'clock.

"Aren't you worried?" Sam asked. "He's been out on the range on an unbroken horse for over three hours."

"I'm a little worried," Brynna admitted, and Sam noticed her stepmother's hand wobbled as she poured a glass of milk. "But I'm not surprised. We were talking last night about how long that horse has been cooped up. After years of freedom, he's spent months in corrals. Wyatt said that as soon as he could, he was going to take Blue out and let him stretch his legs."

If *she'd* done something like that, she would have been grounded for life. Sam considered the unfairness, but decided to stay quiet. Gram had given her the day off from chores so that she could make phone calls to help organize the talent show. She didn't want to do anything to make Gram change her mind.

Two hours later, Sam wasn't so sure that had been a good idea. She'd just finished talking with Rjay, who reported that all of the Journalism students combined had only been able to round up seven acts for the talent show. That meant the chances were good that Mr. Blair would call on them to fill out the list of performers.

But I can't do anything anyone would want to watch, Sam was thinking when she heard Dad stamping dirt from his boots outside.

As he came in, Gram followed, taking off her gardening gloves and sun hat as Dad hung his Stetson on the rack by the front door.

"Sorry to say that horse is a coward," Dad said.

"Nonsense," Gram said. Slipping past Dad, she went about loading three glasses with ice cubes and lemonade as she talked. "You thought the same of Smoke and he turned out fine."

"Smoke wasn't afraid of the cracks in the *playa*, sagebrush movin' in the breeze, or his own shadow."

"His own shadow?" Sam repeated.

Dad nodded. "Took me a while to figure it out, but he's fine in the shade and starts lifting his knees and skittering around, trying not to set his hooves in his shadow as it follows him around."

"Mark my words," Gram said, handing them each a frosty glass. "This time next week you won't believe you said that."

Dad shook his head in disagreement, then said, "We'll see. I'm gonna work him the rest of the day with ropes. Wouldn't hurt you to do a little practice, either," he said to Sam. "Work right where he can see you, and he'll get used to you and the ropes at the same time."

"I might as well," Sam said. "Nothing's going right with this talent show."

"Just the same, we'll be there, won't we, Wyatt?" Gram said. "I think it sounds like a lot of fun."

Dad skipped lunch and went to work accustoming Blue to ropes.

With slow movements, he stripped off the mustang's saddle and rubbed the dampness on his back with a leather riata. Then he returned to some of yesterday's movements, tossing the rope at the horse. At last, he wound the riata through the gelding's legs and pulled it, tickling, past him.

The gelding looked patient, not scared, Sam thought as she worked at roping fence posts. Blue didn't seem to notice her at all and she didn't think he was as far from being ready to work on the cattle drive as Dad thought.

She'd caught the fence post in her loop three times when she suddenly wondered what would have happened if she'd been alone with Jen on the day the bull had attacked.

Could she have roped the bull and used the fence as a pulley to get him off her? If he'd been mounted, Ross probably would have tried that first. And Jake, who was so confident in his roping skills, might have thought of that first.

"Where's Jake when I need him?" Sam didn't know she'd muttered the words aloud until Dad answered her.

"That's the point of being self-sufficient," he said as he let Blue sniff his leather riata.

"I know," Sam said. "Dad?"

"Yeah," he said, hands never still as he worked with the horse.

"Jed doesn't think Jen's self-sufficient, does he?"

"'Course he does," Dad said, flashing her a sharp look as if she were trying to trick him into saying something bad about his friend and neighbor.

"But he's talking about homeschooling her again, not for, you know, academic reasons, but because of this accident."

Even as she said the words, they didn't make sense to her.

"Seems to me that's what you raise kids for, to be independent," Dad said. He walked a few steps away from Blue as the horse drank.

"Do you think he'd be doing this if Jen were a boy?" Sam asked.

Dad shook his head, then caught himself.

"Oh no, I'm not walking into that ambush."

Sam had already seen his answer. He knew Jed's reaction had to do with Jen being a girl.

"Dad, think about it," Sam began, but he was already busy trying to distract her.

Or maybe it was something else, because Dad glanced over at Ross, who'd come to stand at the corral fence.

"I wanta work him around cattle," Dad said. He was talking about Blue, but looking up at the position of the sun. "Ross says he's seen that Hazard bull out at Fishbait Springs again, along with your horse."

Dad meant the Phantom. Sam tried not to be scared. Horses and cattle weren't natural enemies. But there was nothing normal about that bull.

"So first thing tomorrow morning—"

"I—"

Ross blushed as Dad turned to frown at him.

"I th-think now," Ross finished.

Alarm charged through Sam. If Ross thought they should go check on Fishbait Springs now, if he was willing to insist—because even though he'd said "I think," that's what he was doing—then something was seriously wrong.

"Okay," Dad agreed. "We'll kill two birds with one stone. Start gettin' Blue used to stock and investigate those goings-on."

"Okay," Sam said. Before her hands could close

into fists, she stiffened her fingers and told herself she didn't have to be afraid of that bull with Ross and Dad around.

"Take your rope," Dad said, coiling his riata. "You might just get some practice."

Sam shuddered. She couldn't think of anything worse than having that Hazard bull on the end of her rope. Once she caught him, what would she do with him?

By the time Fishbait Springs came into sight, Sam had relaxed a little. Maybe she'd overreacted to Ross's comment. Just because he was quiet and liked to observe the Phantom didn't mean he knew something she didn't.

Sam halted Ace, looped her reins over her saddle horn, and pulled on the sweatshirt she'd tied around her waist. It wasn't cold, but the breeze coming up with the setting sun was brisk.

It was a much longer ride on horseback than it had been in the truck when she'd made the trip with Ross. In fact, she'd been wondering why Dad would make such a long trip so late in the day, until she looked at Ross.

His jaw was set as if something was seriously wrong. Even though she tried to concentrate on Blue, and his easy reaction to cattle, which didn't seem completely new to him, she kept glancing back at Ross.

Ross had told her about the Phantom and the bull

being together at Fishbait Springs. Then he'd told Dad. For a guy like Ross, that came close to insisting they do something.

As they approached the crack-surfaced *playa*, Sam told herself she had to settle down. Ace had begun shying and tossing his head. He must feel her uneasiness.

Blue had walked along calmly until now, but suddenly he began acting like a horse that had only been saddled a few times. He shied at a flying insect, at a bird, at terrors Sam couldn't see.

Lips pressed into a hard line, Dad seemed annoyed with Blue, until he studied Ace. He turned to consider Ross's mount.

"Tank seems fine," Dad observed.

"Always does," Ross said, brushing aside the big bald-faced gelding's calm.

"Think these two know somethin'?" Dad asked, and suddenly Sam remembered her calf Buddy sinking through the crust of the *playa*.

The cracked alkali crust covered an ancient lake, and the sea bed beneath was wetter in some places than in others.

"Like to know if they're right," Dad said in a thoughtful tone.

"Well, I wouldn't," Sam said. Extracting Buddy from the quicksand had been difficult enough. Retrieving a horse and rider would be even worse.

While she and Dad watched the two mustangs'

hooves avoid the same places on the *playa*, Ross must have been looking ahead, because suddenly he pointed.

"No," Dad said.

Sam's eyes scanned wildly across the horizon. What did they see that she was missing? War Drum Flats, a few scattered black rocks, but nothing to sound despairing about the way Dad —

And then she saw them.

The Phantom and the Hazard bull circled each other near the salt grass of Fishbait Springs.

The fact that neither of the animals fled at the approach of riders was proof of their intensity.

Sam had never seen the Phantom stand firm when horsemen were no more than half a mile away.

"That danged Caleb's leaving hay there and those two can't leave it alone," Dad muttered.

He must be right, but to Sam it didn't make sense.

"With all the other food on the range, why would they face off over a few pieces of hay?" she asked.

"Seen two dogs fight over an empty food dish," Ross said.

"Let's leave 'em be," Dad said. "They're likely to work it out better'n us."

Blue jerked at the unfamiliar reins attached to his hackamore, showing a long ivory line of throat. Sam couldn't tell if he was scared or just reacting to all the tension around him.

Suddenly the bull charged. The Phantom squealed, bent his white body into a curve, and his hooves churned, seeming to keep him in one place for far too long.

Sam gasped. All the fear she'd felt for Jen crashed down on Sam again.

Instinctively Ace swung aside, turning her away from skirmish. He was gathering himself to run away.

"No, boy," Sam said, reining him in a circle until he faced the bull and the stallion once more, but he strained against the bit, mouth open.

Sam heard the clap of Ross's heels against Tank's sides an instant before the big gelding jumped into action. Ross's rope was already out as they thundered away.

The singing rope and galloping horse distressed Ace even more.

He sensed danger. He knew he should run. But Sam wouldn't let him.

Surprisingly, Blue paid more attention to his rider. He trembled and rolled his eyes, but he stayed in one place.

Dad had said to wait, but Ross wasn't taking any chances with the Phantom's life. Maybe he was thinking of the last time he'd faced this bull. And Jen.

"He'll handle it," Dad said.

Sam barely heard him. Not satisfied with driving the stallion from the hay, the bull raced after the Phantom.

"Guess we'll see if that crust holds."

It took Sam a few seconds to understand why Dad's voice was so grim. The stallion, the bull, and

Tank, with Ross aboard, were racing to the area Blue and Ace had avoided.

The Phantom ran full out, legs blurring with speed. If the crust wasn't thick enough, his weight would break through first.

Sam leaned forward in her saddle as if she could urge Tank to gallop faster. If Ross roped the bull, the Phantom might sense he was safe and turn aside for better footing.

"Hurry, Ross!" Sam screamed.

Blue reared.

"Cut that out!" Dad snapped.

Was he talking to her or the horse? All Sam knew was that as soon as Blue came back to earth, Dad reached over and grabbed one of her reins near the bit.

She hadn't been about to send Ace dashing after them. Had Dad thought she was?

"There," Dad said, nodding as Ross's loop flared out from his hand like magic. It snared the bull's neck, but the animal didn't stop or even slow. His hind hooves planted. Without losing his balance, the bull spun to face Tank.

The Hazard bull came back at the horse, charging again, with the rope slack between them.

"We need to get two ropes on him," Dad said, sounding too calm. "Hold him between us."

Sam expected Dad to gallop over to help instantly, but he was climbing off his horse.

"I'll need Ace," he said.

She must have stared at him in confusion, even though her mind was catching up before he spoke.

"Not fair to ask this horse to run into that wreck," Dad said. He was already dismounting. "Good boy, Blue. You are one steady horse for a single day of ridin'," Dad said. "And you—" he said firmly, as Ace's hooves pelted the ground in nervous confusion, "straighten up."

Breathing hard, as if she were the one running across the *playa*, Sam dismounted and handed her reins to Dad.

Blue flinched as she took his reins. He snorted, rolled his eyes, and then stopped. Head suddenly higher, ears pricked forward as far as they would go, the Spanish Mustang stared over the *playa*.

"Don't let him go," Dad ordered as he threw himself into her saddle.

"I won't," Sam said. She held the reins with both hands, but she couldn't help following Blue's gaze.

She saw the Phantom take several crashing steps. Water spurted up as it did in the river, but then one of his forelegs disappeared. He plunged ahead with more strength, shoulder muscles straining as he tried to pull the trapped leg along. It almost worked.

For a fleeting second, Sam saw a flash of foreleg—half silver, half mud brown. Then the stallion's hind hooves bit through the crust and his body crashed down. Only his head, neck, and one foreleg showed above the cracked white *playa*.

Chapter Twenty ⌖

A mile across the *playa*, the Phantom was heaving silently in quicksand.

"Don't let him go," Dad repeated, but he didn't mean her stallion. Dad was talking about Blue.

Dad gave the Phantom a single cold-eyed glance and looked back at Sam.

"We'll help him soon as we can. I'm goin' to Ross."

It was only fair that the cowboy came first. He'd just put his own life in danger trying to save the Phantom's.

Ross still held the end of his rope and the bull chased after Tank, but Dad had taken Sam's rope from her saddle. It spun around his head as Ace maneuvered him into position.

Dad would help Ross, but the Phantom wouldn't wait.

"I can't leave him out there," Sam said.

The stallion had stopped struggling, but what did that mean? If the fall hadn't broken his legs, he was just catching his breath. It was ridiculous to think he'd wait patiently for rescue.

And when it came, he'd resist anyone but her.

Sam's fingers touched Dad's long leather riata, coiled neatly on his saddle and snapped in place.

I can't handle it.

If I were a better roper . . .

But she had to handle it. The better ropers were busy trying not to get run down by the Hazard bull. She should wait, but . . .

Suddenly Sam felt sick with the certainty that Ross couldn't go to the Phantom. Tank was a huge Quarter Horse and Ross was a big man. If the Phantom had crashed through the *playa*'s crust, so would they.

Ace was small and light, but with Dad's added weight . . .

Blue was smaller and lighter than the Phantom. Sam was smaller and lighter than Dad. Together, they were the stallion's best hope.

"It's you and me, Blue," Sam told the Spanish Mustang.

Moving gently, crooning constantly, Sam eased her boot into her father's stirrup. She rested her weight there in increasing increments. It wouldn't help the Phantom if she mounted in a hurry and got thrown.

More pressure in the stirrup, a little more, and the Spanish Mustang swung his head around to stare at her. Then, just as he had that first day at Willow Springs, he gave a clownish yawn with his long pink tongue extended.

What are you waiting for? he seemed to ask.

Sam glanced away for a minute, but the blue-and-white mustang wasn't watching Dad and Ross battle the bull. Trembling with eagerness, the mustang watched the Phantom.

"You know he could die out there if you don't help him, don't you, boy?" Keeping her movements as gentle as fear would allow, Sam lifted her right leg over his back and sat lightly in the saddle. And waited.

"Don't explode on me, Blue. I'm the one who brought you cookies, remember?"

The horse was too still beneath her.

She was asking more of him than she had any right to expect. She could only hope kindness counted for something in his mustang mind.

"Can you go for me, boy?" She didn't tighten her legs, didn't use her boot toes to find Dad's too-long stirrups. She just leaned forward from the waist a tiny bit.

Blue stepped out, uneasy at first, but only for a

few steps. Then he swung into his lovely Paso Fino gait. It was amazingly swift and smooth, and the mustang knew where they were going.

He slowed to a walk so quickly, Sam nearly fell.

Then the blue-and-white gelding picked his way across the *playa*, looking down, placing each hoof as if walking on a tightrope.

And then he stopped.

The Spanish Mustang would go no farther.

"That's okay," Sam told the horse, but she wasn't sure what to do next.

Just yards away, the Phantom watched her through his tangled forelock. His brown eyes glowed with hope.

Oh, Zanzibar.

Sam didn't even whisper the words. The Phantom was quiet enough in his half-sunk position, but if he thought she was calling him to her, he might struggle and drop lower.

She was close enough to rope him, but what if she missed? The stallion's fragile trust would be broken and he'd begin struggling all over again.

Even if she did catch him on the first throw, would Blue pull him out?

She glanced toward Fishbait Springs. Dad still hadn't gotten his loop over the bull's head. He was being careful with Ace, trying to get the gelding into the proper position without exposing him to the bull's battering head.

Sam felt one tight instant of fear for Ace, but it disappeared. Dad would take care of him. It was up to her to rescue the Phantom.

There! At last Dad had roped the bull.

He and Ross rode far out, two ropes stretched in straight lines from riders to the neck of the bull.

If Dad saw what she was about to do . . .

No. *When* Dad saw, he would be furious. She'd pay for putting herself and Blue in danger, so she'd better hurry.

Sam loosed Dad's rope from its holder. Blue's ears flicked back, then forward. He'd learned this part and she felt an eagerness rush through him.

"Oh, good boy," Sam told him.

The Phantom looked up at her words and saw the rope.

He feared ropes even more than most wild things did, and it was Linc Slocum's fault, but she'd blame him for it later.

Sam's fingers closed tight around Dad's short rope. If she threw it, she could kiss her bond with her horse good-bye. She might never get this close to him again.

Stop wasting time, Sam told herself.

Seeing the rope in her hands, the stallion plunged. His last leg disappeared. He sunk and Sam heard his chin strike the *playa*.

Her heart was breaking. Of course he'd never trust her again. But what would that matter if he drowned before her eyes?

Beneath her the Spanish Mustang pounced, taking her a few feet closer. Then he stopped as if his hooves had judged the exact thickness of the alkali crust.

Prayerfully, Sam spun the rope over her head. Wrist rolling, she threw.

As the rope sung toward him, the stallion screamed. The sound sliced through her, but as he neighed, he lengthened his neck and the loop fell exactly where it should have.

Now, if only Blue helped. Dad hadn't taught him to back against a weighted rope, so she leaned forward.

The Phantom was silent as the horse pranced past him, as the rope tightened, as he surged against the crust, after the rope and the Spanish Mustang and Sam.

She was so afraid she'd break his legs, but even as Sam thought it, both silver forelegs pawed at the crust.

"Keep going, Blue," Sam whispered.

When she looked back at her horse, Sam heard a shout.

Dad had seen her. She had only seconds, a minute at most, before he came after her. Except, he wouldn't, would he? Dad wouldn't desert Ross with the bull.

The Phantom, too, had heard Dad yell.

With a mighty moan, he lurched, and his front

hooves gained traction on the crust. He pulled, lay for a moment on his left side, and then Blue sprinted a few steps, pulling the stallion up onto his front hooves.

A single second later, the stallion heaved his hindquarters free of the muck, and then he was running. Wobbly and weak, he didn't stop to shake the wet from his coat, or glare at her.

Sam tried to flip Dad's rope loose from the Phantom's neck.

At first she thought she'd done it, but the rope settled over his poll, between his ears, and she let it go.

As the stallion bolted farther off, she realized Dad wouldn't be any madder at her because she'd lost his rope, too.

But she didn't. Sam was still watching the stallion when he paused, shook his head so violently his mane made a silver corona, and then bucked to dislodge the rope.

And then the Phantom was running as he was meant to. Streaked with mud, he headed for the safety of his hidden herd.

There was no rocking, no halting movement in his gait. All four of his legs pumped with power, working to carry him across the *playa* and away from her.

The Spanish Mustang turned to face the oncoming riders, but as soon as he saw the bull lassoed and bucking between them, he began backing away.

"You walk that horse on home slow," Dad shouted above the huffing of the bull.

"Yes, sir," Sam said.

Her gaze moved briefly to Ross. How would she ever thank him? If he hadn't insisted they ride out here . . . if he hadn't galloped Tank after the bull . . .

But Ross's hat was askew and his face gray. Had the bull scared him that much or was she to blame?

"Samantha! Girl, are you listening to me? Don't stop for a single thing."

Sam couldn't remember Dad ever calling her "girl" like that, and she didn't like it.

"I'll just pick up your rope and—"

"Leave it!" Dad bellowed. "Get yourself and my horse on home. I'll deal with you later."

Deal with her? That didn't sound good, either.

"Yes, sir," Sam repeated.

It was full dark by the time she reached River Bend Ranch.

Neighs floated from the ten-acre pasture, and the porch light was on. As Sam and Blue crossed the bridge over the La Charla River, Sam could see both Gram and Brynna standing outside. It looked like their arms were crossed.

Sam sighed. If Dad and Ross had taken the bull back to Jed at River Bend Ranch, they'd probably called from there to tell on her.

All the way home, Sam had replayed her conversation with Dad, in which they'd talked about Jen and her father. Dad had said that the point of raising children was to make them independent. And just the other day Brynna had said parents were supposed to give their children roots and wings. Didn't flying off on her own to save her horse count as wings?

Sam gave an even heavier sigh. She could remind the adults of both those things, but she'd probably better wait awhile.

As she rode Blue past the porch, neither Gram nor Brynna said a word, but that didn't mean she wasn't in trouble. They probably didn't want to spook the horse.

When they reached the round pen, Blue gave her more trouble than he had all evening. Sam felt his back actually hump up beneath the saddle. She remembered Pepper being catapulted from Blue's back, then slamming into the dirt.

She wasn't half as good a rider as Pepper, and she wasn't set up to ride a bucking horse. Her ankles hurt from dangling without stirrups, and the saddle was too big for her. If Blue wanted to buck her off, he would, and then he'd be gone.

Sam was afraid to stay on and afraid to get off.

Life was getting worse by the second.

A few minutes ago she'd been daydreaming that Jed would forgive Ross after he'd brought the Hazard bull home. Now, the only bright thought in her mind was that when Blue got finished with her, she and Jen might end up roommates. In the hospital.

Think like a horse, Sam ordered herself, but it

wasn't easy to read his mind while she was reading his body language.

Blue had enjoyed his taste of freedom. She knew that much.

He wasn't about to return to that corral. He backed against it, slamming the fence with his hindquarters.

"I understand," Sam told him. "But, Blue, that's where you live for now. Maybe in a couple days you can move in with the other horses."

Blue's ears drooped to each side. He took a step forward, then backed into the fence even harder.

Sam glanced at the dark bunkhouse, trying to see a light, or the flicker of the TV screen. Dallas and Pepper were always there and ready to interfere. Where were they when she needed them?

Then she heard voices. Gram and Brynna were arguing on the front porch.

Great, that's just what we need around here, Sam thought.

Then Gram walked toward her, and Sam wondered if that meant Gram had won or lost.

Gram clucked her tongue as she approached and the horse turned his head, but only one ear was cupped toward Gram. Backcast and suspicious, the other ear listened for Sam to do something stupid.

But suddenly, Blue sensed something that made him happy. His tail swished and a low whinny rumbled through his barrel. Sam's legs felt it before she heard it.

"Oh, so you do like oatmeal cookies," Gram sweet-talked the horse as he followed. "That's what I heard."

Gram walked into the round pen ahead of them, and now even Sam could smell the cookies. Oh my gosh. She was starving. It was long past dinnertime, and if the cookies smelled that good to her, she could only imagine Blue's excitement.

Because Dad had started the Spanish Mustang in a bitless hackamore, Blue ate right out of Gram's hand. While he did, Sam eased from the saddle, landing as lightly as possible beside the horse. His head swung around to study her, but then Gram took another cookie from her apron pocket and offered it to him.

Sam closed the gate, then leaned against it with a sigh.

No matter what kind of awful punishment they'd planned for her, Brynna, Dad, and Gram couldn't do anything that would make her feel worse than the Phantom's stare of betrayal as he'd spotted her hurling that rope toward his scarred neck.

"Gram," Sam began.

"Shh," Gram said, and nodded toward the mustang's tack.

Sam's arms trembled by the time she'd hauled Dad's saddle and the hackamore to the tack room. When she saw the empty spot where her own tack went, she recalled the sheet of poems.

It seemed like Ross had left them a month ago, but it had only been a few nights.

He hadn't actually admitted they were his, but of course they were. When she'd suggested he take them to the Cowboy Poetry Gathering in Elko or somewhere they could be appreciated, his expression had been a combination of disappointment and longing.

N-never h-h-happen, Ross had said, but he'd looked like he wanted nothing more. And she could make his dream come true.

"Oh no," Sam said into the silent tack room.

If it was her conscience speaking, it had better get used to being ignored.

And yet the Phantom could have been run down by the bull and injured, if Ross hadn't insisted they go out to Fishbait Springs. And the Phantom had been running in clumsy terror at the bull's first charge, and Ross had ridden at the bull, forgetting he and Tank could have been hit just as easily as the wild silver stallion.

Sam shook her head, trying to jiggle the idea loose.

"No way," she told Blaze as he frisked around her dirty boots while she walked back to the white ranch house. "No way in the whole, wide world."

Chapter Twenty-One ∾

$\mathcal{B}$ackstage at the Darton High School Talent Show, Sam smelled barbecue smoke.

Two days of being confined to her room and ordered to clean every chaotic corner, including her closet, while she thought about how foolhardy she'd been, made even the scent of charred hot dogs blowing in from the grills staffed by the Math Club smell like fresh air.

Through the snagged beige stage curtain, she heard the audience chattering as they chose seats. It sounded like lots of people and that made her feel a little queasy. Or maybe she was just too warm, dressed in jeans, chaps, and a fringed shirt from Gram's closet.

Too bad if Rachel or Daisy sneered about her looking like a cowgirl. Tonight, that's what she wanted people to see.

She used both hands to fan her face.

It was a little better out here than it had been in the dressing room, which barely held the twenty-seven students who'd agreed to perform.

A few of them had still been going through racks and trunks of old costumes, searching for additions to their outfits. Others were crowded in front of two mirrors, putting on makeup or adjusting apparel that ranged from Cammy's pink sequined baton twirler's leotard to the new boy's pristine martial arts outfit. The *gi*, as he called it, was so blindingly white, the freshman boy had actually warned Rachel—who'd finally turned up after missing dress rehearsal—to step back from him while she was applying her crimson lipstick.

Putting on the shocked demeanor of a diva, Rachel had been speechless.

But not Rjay.

"I like that kid's attitude," he'd muttered to Sam. "Bet we won't see any stage fright from him."

Stage fright. That was when Sam had started pushing her way out of the packed dressing room to the openness of backstage.

Not that it was totally empty.

"Someday, probably after I graduate, we'll get a real theater," Daisy complained. Dressed in her cheerleader uniform, she was part of a skit. "I mean, a stage at one end of the cafeteria, with the audience just sitting in folding chairs? Hello? How *country* is that? You won't believe what you'll see when you get out on that stage."

"I can wait," Sam said, but Daisy ignored her.

"The lights will be out, but you'll look over this sea of bobbing heads, because they're all on the same level, and they can't see around each other."

"That's fine with me," Sam said. "But I wish I could check who's out there."

"Uh, maybe the same people who were out there for the barbecue?" Daisy paused at the noise of kids leaving the dressing rooms to gather backstage. "And our parents."

When Sam still looked worried, Daisy gave a long-suffering sigh and towed her downstage by the sleeve. When they were close enough to touch the curtain, Daisy eased the two halves apart just wide enough to peer out.

"Be my guest," she said, inviting Sam to peek at the audience.

At first, Sam noticed that a lot of people—mostly men—stood in the back of the room. Others crab-stepped down the narrow rows, holding programs, deciding where to sit.

Gram sat in the third row, surrounded by her friends. As Sam watched, Gram leaned forward down the row to talk to Lila Kenworthy. Brynna was there, too, looking as crowded and confined as Sam felt.

Sam had really been hoping she'd spot Jen.

She'd talked with her best friend last night. Jen's fever had broken; her soreness had subsided enough that she could walk around; and when Sam told Jen her plan for tonight, she'd vowed to show up. She'd be at the talent show, she promised, even if it meant getting someone to help with a "jail break."

"Forster! Get yourself back here," barked Mr. Blair. "Listen to your stage manager."

Rjay held a clipboard and he was ticking off the names of everyone on his list of performers.

He made a great stage manager, Sam thought. He was organized and energetic. And since he had the power to give fun or boring assignments to the *Darton Dialogue* staff for the rest of the year, at least those cast members were superattentive.

Mrs. Santos was on stage in front of the curtain, welcoming students back to school, ignoring their groans and thanking parents for their support. Then came the cue to begin.

"And now," Mrs. Santos announced, "on with our show!"

The curtain parted, and the first act, a comedy skit performed by four seniors, broke the ice by launching the audience into laughter.

Sam swallowed. This time tomorrow it would all be over. She could do this.

From across the dark stage, Sam saw Rjay give a forceful thumbs-up.

Next, three girls chanted and hopped through an amazing jump-rope routine, dodging, dancing, and exchanging places amid whirring, whipping ropes.

Sam looked away. Was anyone as nervous as she was? Her stomach might as well be filled with cold lava. Of course there was no such thing, but what was this sluggish, oozing feeling? Should she have eaten one of the Math Club's charred black hot dogs?

Stop it, Sam told herself. She only felt hemmed in by all the people and stage props.

Right, so why were her hands shaking, rattling the pages she had to read soon? Why was there sweat on her forehead and why, no matter how often she swallowed, was she so thirsty?

Of course this was the best way to thank Ross for saving the Phantom. The big cowboy's eyes had filled with appreciation when she told him she'd like to read his poetry for the talent show, but if she couldn't read when the curtain parted and she took her place across the pretend campfire from Ally and her guitar, he'd start wishing she'd just baked him some brownies, instead.

Just then Ally handed her a plastic bottle of water. Sam took it, smiled through the dimness, and drank deeply.

Ally wore a long buttery brown dress that was supposed to look like deerskin. Even though she couldn't see her partner well, Sam could tell Ally was excited as she leaned over to whisper, "You know what the cure for stage fright is, don't you?"

Sam shook her head "no."

"Picture the audience sitting there in their underwear."

Ally had spoken so quietly, it took Sam a second to understand what she'd said, and then she giggled.

Daisy whirled around with her index finger over her lips. Sam choked back her laughter. Daisy's stern look could only mean that Rachel was on stage.

Rachel hadn't shown up for any rehearsals, but Rjay hadn't barred her from performing.

"It's your funeral," he'd told Rachel, but the rich girl had shrugged off his warning.

She'd talked Cammy into setting up her props and playing her accompaniment on a portable sound system. Now Rachel was out there singing, and Sam had to admit, she was pretty good.

Rjay wasn't impressed. He'd maneuvered himself to a place at Sam's elbow.

"She sings like she doesn't want to smear her lip gloss," he said, and Sam knew what he meant.

Rachel's voice was trained and pretty, but it floated away like a balloon on the wind. She didn't put her heart into it, unlike Ally.

Sam glanced at Ally as she lowered her head, hair brushing the guitar strings as she plucked one quietly and listened.

Ally had suggested a way to soothe Sam's nerves, by framing her recitation with a song. They'd appear on the stage together, but Ally would perform first, singing a beautiful song called "Mariah." She'd sing all but the last verse. Then, while Ally played the song on her guitar, Sam would read Ross's poems. When she finished, Ally would complete her song and they'd escape the stage together.

"It's a good thing we decided not to make this a competition," Daisy hissed over the thunderous applause that followed Rachel's performance.

On a wave of perfume and pride, Rachel came offstage as Sam and Ally got ready to go on.

Nervous as she was, Sam couldn't help noticing that for once Rachel was dressed like a high school girl instead of a model and she looked great. Sam decided she should say so. Before she could, Cammy appeared.

"They loved you," Cammy gushed to Rachel as the applause followed her offstage.

"Pearls before swine," Rachel said, brushing back a wave of coffee-colored hair.

"I don't—?" Cammy began, and when Rjay explained that Rachel meant the audience wasn't capable of appreciating her performance, Cammy actually looked surprised.

Sam was still determined to say something nice about Rachel's jeans, floaty blue top, and matching leather flip-flops.

"You look nice," Sam managed to say. "Pretty and simple."

Maybe *simple* had been the wrong thing to say. Sam braced herself for Rachel's retort, but the rich girl just gave a slight, shiny smile.

"Simplicity is the most expensive sort of elegance, you know," Rachel said. Then she glanced at Sam's costume from boot toes to blouse and added, "No, probably you don't."

Sam realized she didn't care what Rachel thought of her. She really didn't.

The jab of Rachel's words was blunted by the fact that Sam always knew what to expect from her.

This time last year they would have hurt, but Sam wasn't a newcomer anymore. This was her school and she had just as much right to be here—however she looked—as anyone else.

For some reason an image of Blue, being brave when he wanted to, not when it was expected of him, popped into Sam's mind. Most people would think it was ridiculous to take a lesson from a horse, but not Sam.

"Our turn," Ally said, touching Sam's back.

The first thing she noticed when she stepped onto the stage was the faint glow of lights in the back, around a refreshments window.

She froze as she saw Dad and Jed standing next to Ross. Together.

"Sam," Ally whispered.

She nodded, but as she found her place, Sam celebrated the fact that Jed Kenworthy and Ross were actually standing side by side. That had to mean Jed had forgiven Ross, didn't it?

"Way out West, they have a name for wind and rain and fire," Ally sang.

Sam glanced into the audience. She saw that Ally had them hypnotized already. She also saw Mrs. Ely and Jake and someone standing next to him, almost hidden by his broad shoulders.

Sam's spirits soared along with Ally's voice when she saw Jen, bracketed and protected between Ryan and Jake.

Jen lifted her chin and gingerly raised her arm in an okay sign, and warm relief washed over Sam as Ally's voice faded and the simple strumming of her guitar meant it was Sam's turn.

"'Alkali Pegasus.'" Sam's voice cracked a little as she read the title of the first poem, but after that, everything was easy.

After "Alkali Pegasus," she read "Valentine from a Hired Hand." Ross had insisted she leave River Bend Ranch out of the title. He didn't want anyone to guess he was the poet.

"'Speak for the silent.'" Sam read the last line of "Echo" and bowed her head. As Ally recommenced singing, Sam felt good.

It had been hard, but she'd thanked Ross for saving her horse, and he deserved this celebration, even if no one else knew about it.

As the last notes of "Mariah" drifted away, applause surrounded Sam and Ally. Offstage, they hugged each other.

"Thank you!" Sam said with all the enthusiasm she could put into her voice.

"No, thank *you*!" Ally insisted. "You were amazing!"

"*You* were amazing," Sam told her, just before something struck her between the shoulder blades.

"Sorry, but I'm on! Out of the way! Go have your hug-fest somewhere else."

It was Zeke, dressed in short leather pants with suspenders. They were called something like lederhosen, Sam thought, and he was carrying his skateboard under one arm.

"What in the world?" Ally said as Zeke maneuvered his way past, still talking.

"Excuse me. Stand back." Zeke paused to make a half bow. Then he wiggled his eyebrows at Daisy and announced, "Make way for the Yodeling Board Man. Darton High School has never seen anything like him!"

"And isn't that lucky," Daisy said, but as Zeke sailed out onto the stage, Sam heard the cheerleader laughing.

With her own part in the show finished, Sam escaped. She made her way through the wings and down the stairs, to stand outside the theater.

She faced the parking lot where even the oldest cars were polished by overhead lights and a full moon.

Finally alone, Sam eased a poem Ross had given her last night from her pocket.

"Read it when you're all done," he'd said.

There'd been no tremor in his voice, but she'd known this poem wasn't for anyone else.

She unfolded the sheet of paper and read the title aloud: "'Sam's Stallion.'"

She closed her eyes for a minute, hoping the Phantom was still hers, hoping she hadn't saved his life and lost his love.

She opened her eyes and read the poem in a whisper.

> *"He's called a phantom*
> *But his tracks never grow dim*
> *Around here, 'round her."*

Sam turned the horsehair bracelet three turns around her wrist before she folded the letter and slipped it back into her pocket. Maybe she should have waited. Maybe she should have read it while standing beside the La Charla, so she could watch the wild side of the river.

If Ross was right, the Phantom would still come around. They'd still see each other, if only from a distance.

Sam took a deep breath, tilted her head back, and looked up toward the black-and-silver sky.

Tonight, she and her stallion were together under one moon. For now, that was enough.

From
Phantom Stallion
  21

DAWN RUNNER

Glossy Shetland ponies crowded together in the late afternoon shade of cottonwood trees. Standing head to tail, they whisked breezes over each other's faces as if nothing were wrong.

For them, it wasn't, but Samantha Forster was worried. How could something she'd wished for bring bad luck to the wild horses she loved?

The early September sun sizzled against Sam's back. Summer hadn't ended just because it was the first day of school.

She glanced toward the mansion sitting atop the man-made hill overlooking Gold Dust Ranch. The oversized house was air-conditioned and after the long walk from the school bus stop to visit her best friend, that refrigerated air would feel wonderful.

But her best friend lived in the foreman's house, not the mansion. Sam knew she was more likely to receive an invitation from the ponies, to share their irrigated emerald pasture, than one into Linc Slocum's giant pillared house.

She'd worn a knit shirt Gram had called adobe red, and a denim skirt, because Gram and Brynna, her stepmother, had ganged up on her until she'd accepted their claim that she only had one chance to make a good impression on her teachers during this first week of school. But it was too warm for the sunny afternoon, especially when she was carrying two sets of books.

Fretting over the temperature made a nice change from replaying last night's phone call.

Forget about the heat and the phone call, Sam told herself as she knocked at the front door of the small foreman's house near Gold Dust Ranch's front gates. But she couldn't.

At first she'd been so excited. Pam O'Malley, her best friend from San Francisco, was coming to Nevada. Right this minute, Pam and her mom should be driving their camper from the city to Lost Canyon. Sam was excited to see Pam again and she couldn't wait for her old best friend to meet her new one, but then Pam had announced the reason for their trip.

"My mom has a grant to study mythological horses and write a paper about them," Pam had explained. "She's going to investigate the wild horses around your area, and focus on stories of some legendary stallion."

The only legendary stallion in northern Nevada was the Phantom. Sam knew that as well as she knew the mustang's safety depended on staying hidden, not being put under a magnifying glass.

Sam knocked a second time, then fluttered the neck of her blouse for coolness while she waited for Jennifer Kenworthy, her best friend in the entire world, to let her in out of the sun. Level-headed Jen would help her figure out what to do about Pam and her mother. Jen's passion was complex mathematics, and she loved solving intricate problems of any kind.

But Sam didn't have time to announce her news.

"Stay out," Jen said as soon as she saw Sam.

She didn't sound angry, just firm as she slipped past the screen door to come outside.

Jen's white-blond braids were pinned haphazardly atop her head and her arm moved a little stiffly as it brushed aside the day's homework Sam carried with her.

A week ago, an attack by a range bull had shattered one of Jen's ribs. According to her parents, Jen wasn't well enough yet to return to school, so Sam had brought her new books to her.

With her torso still wrapped for protection, Jen stepped gingerly off the porch. Sam stepped back to let Jen ease past.

"What's up?" Sam asked.

"Nothing that'll make you happy," Jen said as she led the way across the silently baking ranch yard.

Sam felt her worry double.

As she left the stack of books and homework on the porch, she wondered if Jen's parents had decided their daughter should go back to being homeschooled instead of attending Darton High.

No, a silent voice wailed in Sam's head, but she just crossed her fingers and hoped not. Since Jen's accident, the idea had been under discussion. The last Sam had heard, though, Jen's parents were still locked in disagreement.

"C'mon," Jen said, looking back over her shoulder. "I want you to look at something."

With a sigh of relief, Sam followed. You couldn't look at a decision.

As she fell into step beside her friend, Sam almost blurted out her worries over Pam, but she knew she should be considerate first.

"How does your rib feel?" Sam asked.

"Like the broken ends of that bone are still grating together under my skin," Jen grumbled. "And don't get me started on wearing layers of protective bandages during a heat wave."

Then Jen gave a lopsided grin, probably so Sam wouldn't think she was whining.

Sam shuddered. Heat and sweat she could tolerate, but she winced at her friend's pain. When she opened her mouth to sympathize, Jen stopped her.

"Talking about it is a waste of time."

"Right," Sam said, then turned her head so Jen wouldn't see her smile.

Jen's injury hadn't smothered her take-charge attitude.

"What are you going to show me?" Sam asked. Despite everything, excitement bounced up in her when she noticed they were headed for Gold Dust Ranch's modern barn. The barn meant horses.

"No hints," Jen muttered. "I want your honest assessment. Maybe Ryan and I are overreacting."

Sam took a deep breath. Telling Jen about Pam's visit would have to wait.

Ryan Slocum, whose father owned the Gold Dust Ranch, was new to Nevada and he sometimes misunderstood the Western way of things. But Jen had been born on this ranch. If Sam added all Jen's experience to the fact that she was a science and math whiz who insisted on a logical explanation for everything, the chances that Jen was overreacting were pretty small.

Sam squinted and blinked as she passed from the glaring sunlight into the dim barn. Before her eyes accustomed themselves to the change, Jen shushed her.

"Wha—?" Sam managed before she made out the index finger Jen had raised to her lips, then pointed.

Sam looked toward the barn's biggest box stall,

but it was empty.

The quiet only lasted a second.

Ryan Slocum's voice sliced through it. Squinting her dazzled eyes, Sam made him out, standing near a wall-mounted telephone.

"Pardon me," he said, to whoever listened on the other end of the line, but he didn't sound apologetic. "I don't mean to be too direct, but I've been waiting— no, it's not an emergency. Not exactly. You see, this is my second call to Dr. Scott and I've yet to hear . . ."

Sam stiffened. Dr. Scott was the nearest veterinarian. If Ryan had phoned the vet twice, something must be seriously wrong. And it must be about Shy Boots, the colt Ryan loved.

"Yes, actually, I've been concerned for several days," Ryan continued. "However, I've driven the distance between—" Ryan's lecturing tone broke off and he flinched. "Oh, I see, a pet tortoise hit by a car. That's dreadful." Ryan sighed. "Well then, I suppose there's nothing to do except wait. You've been quite helpful," Ryan added, and then he hung up and turned toward Sam.

"What's wrong with Shy Boots?" Sam blurted.

Seeing that her plan for an impartial evaluation was doomed, Jen said, "He won't get up."

"Won't or can't?" Sam asked. Although she'd never seen the problem, she'd heard of "cast" horses who got wedged in weird positions in their stalls and couldn't gather themselves to rise.

"See for yourself," Ryan said, walking closer to the box stall.

It turned out not to be empty. When Sam peered inside and saw the Appaloosa foal lying flat on his side, she instantly forgot the sunshine outside. In here, it might as well be November.

The chocolate-brown colt with his hip blanket of white spots wasn't unconscious. His eyes were open, but there was no luster beyond those impossibly long eyelashes.

Listless and still, he watched the humans stare down at him.

Ryan slipped inside the stall and squatted beside Shy Boots. The colt seemed limp. His only movement was a slight flinch away from the stroking of Ryan's hand against his dark velvety neck.

Ryan was the sort of guy who tried to hide his emotions, but Sam could tell his love for the Appaloosa foal made him as anxious as a father.

He didn't even look like himself. His dark hair was disheveled. His pressed khaki pants were smeared with—nope, she wasn't seeing things—a little horse manure.

Sam rarely understood what Jen saw in Ryan Slocum, her almost-boyfriend.

Right now, though, Ryan was so concerned for his colt, he didn't care about his appearance, and Sam wanted to pat him on the back.

"Boots won't leave his stall and his appetite has

slacked off dramatically," Ryan said without looking up at Sam.

"Ryan's checked for a temperature," Jen added, "but the thermometer reads right at one hundred degrees." Jen gave Sam an owlish glance. "And that's normal."

"Okay," Sam said. "Could he have hurt himself? Just pulled a tendon and be feeling crummy?"

"There's no sign of trauma or swelling." Jen bit her lip. Jen planned to study veterinary medicine in college and she'd already started looking at animals as patients. Above the nosepiece of her glasses, her frown deepened. "I've thought of West Nile virus, but I can't find any insect bite and I'm not up on all the symptoms—"

"Jen," Sam interrupted. "Why don't we wait for the vet?"

"It could be a while, and I can't even enjoy the satisfaction of feeling angry. Not without being a brute," Ryan said. "You heard what I said about the tortoise being backed over by a car?"

The girls nodded, grimacing.

"I'm sure Boots is fine," Jen said, trying to sound casual. "But the poor little guy's been through so much."

Sam took a deep breath, but when she exhaled, she felt no relief. Jen was right.

Sired by a rogue stallion named Diablo and mothered by Hotspot, a young mare who'd escaped before she could become the cornerstone of Gold Dust Ranch's Appaloosa breeding program, Shy Boots had been unwanted before he was even born.

Soon after the mare and foal had survived a difficult birth, Linc Slocum had tried to wean Shy Boots early.

That was one of the rare times that Ryan, whose heart had been won by the two horses, had stood up to his father. Ryan had objected to the early separation, and so had Hotspot. Although she'd been purchased solely as a broodmare, Hotspot had refused to mate with a stallion whose high-priced bloodlines matched her own.

Just days later, Ryan had overheard Linc's plan to solve the problem by destroying Hotspot's "mongrel" foal.

Before that could happen, the horses had been stolen, then separated. Luckily, the inept thief hadn't taken the horses too far away. Hotspot had joined the Phantom's herd and Shy Boots had been found at a petting zoo, where he'd been adopted by a burro foster mother. But that arrangement had been temporary.

Now, with Hotspot still out on the range, the colt was alone again.

Jen was right. The little guy had been through a lot.

"Maybe he's just tired and overwhelmed," Sam suggested.

"He's not eating, even though I offer him the bottle all the time, now," Ryan said. Something in his tone sounded a little guilty, and Sam could guess why.

When Jen had been in the hospital, Ryan had spent hours driving back and forth to Darton. Then he sat in a chair at her beside, talking. Jen had appreciated his company, but who had fed Shy Boots?

Ryan was an excellent rider, but had he ever been responsible for the daily care of his own horse? In England, there had been grooms and trainers to monitor his horses' health. Did he know foals needed frequent feeding, even when humans thought they had more important things to do?

Before she could bring up the touchy subject, they all heard a faint mechanical whirr, then a clang as the iron gates to Gold Dust Ranch opened and closed.

From his bed of straw, Shy Boots' dark ears twitched, picking up the sound of an approaching truck.

"That will be Dr. Scott," Ryan said, and Sam saw him return to being his usual self.

With brisk movements, he stood, brushed at his soiled pants, and left the stall.

He tossed back his dark hair and shed the worry that had bowed him over the foal. As Ryan made his way toward the vet, his manner said he wasn't the sort of guy who liked to be kept waiting.

Read all the Phantom Stallion Books!

#1: The Wild One
Pb 0-06-441085-4

#2: Mustang Moon
Pb 0-06-441086-2

#3: Dark Sunshine
Pb 0-06-441087-0

#4: The Renegade
Pb 0-06-441088-9

#5: Free Again
Pb 0-06-441089-7

#6: The Challenger
Pb 0-06-441090-0

#7: Desert Dancer
Pb 0-06-053725-6

#8: Golden Ghost
Pb 0-06-053726-4

#9: Gift Horse
Pb 0-06-056157-2

www.phantomstallion.com

#10: Red Feather Filly
Pb 0-06-056158-0

#11: Untamed
Pb 0-06-056159-9

#12: Rain Dance
Pb 0-06-058313-4

**#13: Heartbreak
Bronco**
Pb 0-06-058314-2

#14: Moonrise
Pb 0-06-058315-0

#15: Kidnapped Colt
Pb 0-06-058316-9

**#16: The Wildest
Heart**
Pb 0-06-058317-7

#17: Mountain Mare
Pb 0-06-075845-7

#18: Firefly
Pb 0-06-075846-5

#19: Secret Star
Pb 0-06-075847-3

AVON BOOKS
An Imprint of HarperCollinsPublishers